Fearless Female
SOLDIERS, EXPLORERS, AND AVIATORS

Amelia Earhart

FIRST WOMAN TO FLY SOLO ACROSS THE ATLANTIC

KRISTIN THIEL

Cavendish Square
New York

Published in 2018 by Cavendish Square Publishing, LLC
243 5th Avenue, Suite 136, New York, NY 10016

First Edition

Library of Congress Cataloging-in-Publication Data

Names: Thiel, Kristin, 1977- author.
Title: Amelia Earhart : first woman to fly solo across the Atlantic / Kristin Thiel.
Description: New York : Cavendish Square Publishing, [2018] |
Series: Fearless female soldiers, explorers, and aviators |
Includes bibliographical references and index.
Identifiers: LCCN 2017000103 (print) | LCCN 2017001596 (ebook) |
ISBN 9781502627490 (library bound) | ISBN 9781502627506 (E-book)
Subjects: LCSH: Earhart, Amelia, 1897-1937–Juvenile literature. |
Air pilots–United States–Biography–Juvenile literature. |
Women air pilots–United States–Biography–Juvenile literature.
Classification: LCC TL540.E3 T495 2018 (print) | LCC TL540.E3 (ebook) |
DDC 629.13092 [B] –dc23
LC record available at https://lccn.loc.gov/2017000103

Editorial Director: David McNamara
Editor: Stacy Orlando
Copy Editor: Nathan Heidelberger
Associate Art Director: Amy Greenan
Designer: Stephanie Flecha
Production Coordinator: Karol Szymczuk
Photo Research: J8 Media

The photographs in this book are used by permission and through the courtesy of: Cover, Everett Historical/Shutterstock.com; pp. 4, 11, 21, 38, Bettmann/Getty Images; pp. 10, 106 Underwood Archives/Archive Photos/Getty Images; p. 17 Jordan McAlister/Moment/Getty Images; p. 23 Austrian Archives/Imagno/Getty Images; p. 24 FPG/Getty Images; p. 29 © Corbis/Getty Images; p. 37 User: Eyetooeye, Own work/File: Neta Snook and Mr- Pratt in 1922 in Long Beach, California- Pratt is my great grandfather who was good friends with Miss Snook 2014-07-10 10-33.jpg /Wikimedia Commons; p. 43 Pictorial Press Ltd/Alamy Stock Photo; p. 44 en: User: Bzuk uploaded it to wikipedia, User: Alaniaris re-uploaded it to Commons/File: Neta amelia kinner airster s.jpg/Wikimedia Commons; pp. 52, 81 George Rinhart/Corbis/Getty Images; p. 60 File: Oceania-map 1-41000000.jpg/Wikimedia Commons; p. 63 RNGS/RTR/Newscom; p. 73 AP Photo/Charles Tasnadi; p. 75 Imaginechina/AP Images; p. 78 NY Daily News/Getty Images; p. 85 Anton Bruehl/Condé Nast /Getty Images; p. 86 AP/Photo/J. Pat Carter; p. 89 adoc-photos/Corbis/Getty Images; p. 91 AP Photo; p. 94 Stephane De Sakutin/AFP/Getty Images; p. 100 AP Photo/Doug Pizac; p. 107 photo courtesy of Air Race Classic, Inc. All rights reserved; p. 108 NASA/File: Whitson greets Melroy.jpg/Wikimedia Commons; p. 112 Spc. Jessica Nemec/File: Apache pilot leads the way 150326-Z-OX391-001.jpg/Wikimedia Commons.

Printed in the United States of America

Contents

one

Amelia Earhart's Corner of the World

"Flying would eventually define her, it would bring her unheard-of fame, and in time it would lead to her famous disappearance, one of the greatest mysteries in the history of the United States" **—W. C. Jameson**

The phrase that describes Amelia Earhart in her senior-year high school yearbook is: "The girl in brown who walks alone." Exactly what the writer meant by that is lost to history, but we can look back on Earhart's life and read the line as a simple, powerful description of her. As a curious child, Earhart was constantly doing her own thing, while her family's

Opposite: Amelia Earhart was a famous airplane pilot who met the challenges of flying and celebrity head on.

frequent moves kept her the new kid in school. She grew up to be a pioneer in her career, and she died in a remote corner of the world, doing the unique work she loved.

During Earhart's time, there were a lot of restrictions and challenges for women and others who were trying to break outside of society's constraints. In the early 1900s, also known as the early twentieth century, there were different rules for men versus women, for those of different ethnic groups, and for those of different socioeconomic classes. Many lives were stymied because of the laws and expectations of the times, but other strong and remarkable people were able to succeed. Earhart's story is one in which she pressed forward and overcame the odds, even though her passion brought her to a mysterious end.

The Haunting Allure of Amelia Earhart

Almost eighty years after she was proclaimed dead, people continue to pose theories about Earhart. Why her story has had such a strong and lasting hold on the public may be an even greater mystery than her final journey. "Now that she's long gone, why are people holding onto this?" wondered Dorothy Cochrane, a curator at the National Air and Space Museum, in a *Smithsonian* magazine article. People who never met her, who may not have even lived during her time, express intense feelings about her, some positive, some negative. Many of the theories surrounding her death offer troubling rumors of Earhart. Some claim she was an incompetent pilot, and others accuse her of being a spy. Furthermore, as new evidence is found, many have changed their opinions about her. With the emergence of new information, some who had once been Earhart's critics now express relief at being able to look fondly upon her. Earhart seems to feel as real as a family member to many people, the circumstances of her final flight as newsworthy as if they had transpired today.

Earhart has received the same attention anyone with major celebrity does: some people love her, and some dislike her; some admire and respect her; and some don't understand why she is considered such a mythic figure. In some ways, it is not surprising that she has come to overshadow other trailblazers in her field. She was born with a lot of social and economic advantages. She was white at a time when race mattered a lot. Though her family didn't always have money, they came from it, and they always seemed to find a way out of tough spots. These advantages helped her attend school, pay for flying classes, and buy airplanes. She also went on to marry into money and prestige.

Earhart was charismatic, charming those around her and not shying from the spotlight. Earhart may have grown up a "plain Jane," but people gravitated toward her style once she was an adult. She was featured in magazine photo spreads and had her own fashion line. Still, hers is a story as much about celebrity and the life cycle of myth as it is about the early days of **aviation** and the first **aviators**.

As we move just a little closer to understanding Earhart's story, which may never offer all the answers we crave, it may be best to keep in mind what then Secretary of State Hillary Clinton said about a major search for Earhart that kicked off in 2012: "Even if you do not find what you seek, there is great honor and possibility in the search itself." When thinking about such a "needle in a haystack" adventure—as the oceanographer who found the *Titanic* and *Bismark* shipwrecks called looking for Earhart's last plane—that may be the best attitude to hold.

Being Different Just Made Sense!

Today, we see Earhart as someone who shattered glass ceilings. As a girl and then as a woman, she did things that society did not consider very feminine. Some of her feats were fantastic for any human, let alone females. It is, after all, quite daring to pilot your own plane, especially back in the days when air travel was new and experimental. We look up to her, call her brave, and say she took a stand against convention and sexism. Yet Earhart often took a logical view of her bold choices. Even though it can be said that the decisions she made were progressive, they just made common sense to her.

Take, for example, one time when she went sledding down a snowy hill in Atchison, Kansas. In the early 1900s, there were guidelines about what was acceptable behavior for girls, and a different set of rules for boys. These parameters applied to nearly everything, including sledding. Boys were permitted to lie down on their sleds, but girls were expected to sit while hurtling down hillsides. Ladies don't sprawl! As we'll see throughout this book, Earhart rarely followed such rules. They did not make sense to her, and in the case of at least this sled ride, they were downright dangerous. She wrote about it later:

> I was zipping down one of the really steep hills in town when a junk man's cart, pulled by a horse with enormous blinders, came out from a side road. The hill was so icy that I couldn't turn and the junk man didn't hear the squeals of warning. In a second my sled had slipped between the front and back legs of the horse and got clear, before either he or I knew what had happened. Had I been sitting up, either my head or the

horse's ribs would have suffered in contact—probably the horse's ribs.

In other words, had she been sledding like a so-called proper lady, there would have been injuries.

Earhart experienced less dramatic moments that were nonetheless just as hindered by gender-specific restrictions. In her autobiography, Earhart wrote, "Whether or not [women] are fitted to do what men do physically remains to be seen." This was not because women didn't want to participate in athletics, but because they weren't allowed to do so on ground even with men. Earhart rode bicycles and played basketball and tennis, but because she was female, she received no formal instruction. She felt, therefore, that her skill and grace could never possibly match her passion, no matter how hard she tried. She also argued that the very clothing for women and girls prevented them from doing their best, as their dress was so restrictive and impractical.

Fashion Rules—and the Ways Earhart Broke Them

Women's fashion of the early 1900s has been called "extremely lavish and cumbersome." Women wore long, heavy skirts and puffy, lacy blouses. The desired figure was an S shape, with skirts cut to hug the hips and flare at the hem, suited more for a mermaid than a human. In 1908, the drama of frills was replaced with tailored suits, blouses, and skirts. Throughout, however, women's undergarments remained the same. Whether they were to wear fussy skirts or crisply cut suits, women had to also wear the constricting **corset**.

A corset is a laced bodice that is cinched to pull the torso in and up. It has been worn for centuries (and can still be

Women had to dress up even when bicycling, a popular activity for women in the early 1900s.

found today), but it reached its height of popularity for daily use in the 1800s. In 1900, Inès Gaches-Sarraute, who had studied medicine and recognized the health problems the extremely binding nineteenth-century corsets could cause, presented the "health corset." It removed pressure from the waist and diaphragm, yes, but it ended up pushing the breasts forward and the hips back. Even while bicycling, women were forced to wear this constrictive secret.

Not long before Earhart's birth in 1897, girls were dressed like little women. Into the 1880s, starting from nine years of age, girls wore fitted bodices on top and skirts that draped over bustles, which extended their backsides. In the 1890s, girls' clothing got much simpler, in part because little girls were allowed to be more active than they had been previously. During the same decade of Earhart's birth, people started to understand that crawling was an important stage in physical and mental human development, but babies, boys and girls alike, had been outfitted in short dresses, not really appropriate for a lot of on-the-ground crawling. So parents added one-piece rompers, called "creeping aprons," as cover-ups. Even though girls were not supposed to wear pants, at least these were acceptable.

Pink and blue were associated with gender by the 1910s, though in the opposite order than we think of them today. This was because pink was seen as a light shade of red, the color of Mars, the god of war, and a stronger color for boys. Meanwhile, blue was associated with Venus, the goddess of love, or the Madonna, a representation of Jesus's mother Mary, and was seen as a delicate color for girls. This reversed in the 1940s.

When Earhart could choose her clothes as an adult, she dressed, for the most part, decidedly unfrilly and uncinched. She even made her own clothes, and she did not wear any items that would enhance her features or change the appearance of her figure to fit more into the conventional notions of beauty. Even for formal events that she was the guest of honor at, such as White House dinners, **ticker-tape parades**, and lectures, she leaned toward neutral colors and

In 1932, President Herbert Hoover presented the National Geographic Society gold medal to Amelia Earhart.

flowing lines allowing for motion. Her best clothes, reserved for those cases, were layered and loose dresses, and outfits without a lot of rigid structure. She just as frequently was seen in public in her flight gear: a jumpsuit or **jodhpurs**; lace-up knee boots; a white shirt; a man's tie; a bomber jacket or a leather coat. Her look was not flashy, sometimes considered manly, and more often than not unisex.

Earhart's most extreme bucking of fashion expectation was in an area that the public was unable to see: she wore men's underpants when she flew. It feels fitting that Earhart refused to be constricted even in her undergarments and rebelled against the restricting corset! She maintained that she found men's underwear easier to adjust for a quick pee than women's underwear (and probably practical on long flights). To layer on the scandal, it's said that she was given the gift of two other people's underwear for her to wear: her husband donated boxers, and her lover gave her a pair of his briefs.

Teaching Gender Expectations

With the gender-based rules of the day, young people learned more at school than just "the three Rs," the so-called basics of education: reading, writing, and arithmetic. Students witnessed and received examples of men being allowed to do things that women were not. For instance, teachers who were women, as most at the time were, had curfews and were not allowed to spend time with male friends. Even if they were in a relationship, they were not allowed to marry while employed by a school. One list of rules from 1915 explained that women teachers could not smoke cigarettes, wear bright colors, dye their hair, leave the city without permission from the school board, or even hang out in ice cream shops downtown.

Teaching was one of the few accepted professions for women. Because women were considered nurturers, they were seen as fitting teachers. Most teachers were therefore women, and the profession carried less prestige and a lower salary than comparable work. In some ways, the fact that women could have a career at all offered a possibility for independence. They could earn their own money, which meant they might have been able to make some choices not available to those women who didn't work outside the home. In other ways, women in the profession were acting out the roles they already played at home, becoming second mothers to their students. This was limited freedom however, as they were kept under the forceful thumbs and watchful eyes of male administrators and town leaders.

The "Weaker" Sex

Despite proof to the contrary, women were considered the weaker sex. Women demonstrated physical strength and ability daily, not just bearing children but also performing quite demanding domestic duties, such as washing heavy clothes and linens by hand, drawing water and carrying it back home, tending animals, and manual farm work.

Women living under the control of men was not something unique to Earhart's time. Societal norms and laws had long separated the sexes. Women were supposed to be wives and mothers, and if they didn't get married and have children, they were considered **spinsters**, old maids, or even barren witches. Without a career outside the home, a single woman could not make money to support herself, forcing her to be reliant on someone in her life who did have money, usually her father or another male relative. A woman who didn't have a husband and children was somehow invisible in, threatening to, and draining on society—all three at once.

Married women were constrained by society's rules as well. As far back as the Roman Empire, early law decreed women as children, forever inferior to men. This was the case in early America, too. Men owned women and children. They could send children to poorhouses without their wives' consent; they could commit their wives to mental asylums without their consent. A woman had to seek her husband's permission for everything.

What's more, women could not make choices about family or children. In 1873, the Comstock Act passed, prohibiting advertisements and other information about and distribution of birth control, and allowing the postal service to confiscate birth control sold through the mail. In 1916, Margaret Sanger opened the first birth control clinic in the United States. Within the year, this would be considered "a public nuisance," and she was arrested and jailed for the first of many times to come. Religion played an even bigger role in family planning than it does today, with many denominations forbidding birth control or expecting women to raise more children to join God's flock.

While religion held women to the roles of wife and mother, women were also, somewhat conversely, associated with evil and temptation. In Judeo-Christian society, the most famous example of this is Eve, who was blamed for bringing original sin to humans. Pandora, from Greek mythology, opened a forbidden box and brought plagues and unhappiness to mankind. Still today, we say that making a misstep can open Pandora's box and cause a cascade of problems.

The cycle continued both in the classroom and at home, with mothers instructing daughters to conform to these expectations. As late as the 1960s, tests showed that while girls did well academically in elementary school, their achievement lessened by high school. Researchers have theorized that because no one expected anything of the girls beyond marriage and motherhood, they lost interest and gave up on studying. As an adult, Earhart would speak on the importance of education and again call on her unique brand of logic. In a speech to Barnard College students on May 8, 1931, she criticized the educational system for being founded on "sex, not aptitude." This discriminatory system simply made no sense to Earhart: "I know a great many boys who should be making pies—and a great many girls who would be better off in manual training."

Succeeding Without Role Models

It is amazing that Earhart could appear so determined and sure about her choices and her lifestyle. Society had different expectations for women and men, and there were not many role models, of either gender, demonstrating how to break out of the norm. In addition, Earhart did not have female role models in **aeronautics** because the female pioneers in flying were coming up in the industry at the same time she was, more or less. In fact, the aeronautics pioneers, male and female alike, were all starting around the same time.

Today, many young adults in the United States are told they can do anything. A college degree has become nearly as

Earhart's Birthplace: A Leader in Trade and Communication

Earhart spent her childhood in the Midwest, a part of the United States that is consistent in at least one thing: extreme weather conditions. Earhart could count on hot, sticky summers and icy, snowy winters as her family moved from state to state within the region. She was born in 1897 in Atchison, Kansas. When she was ten, the family moved to Des Moines, Iowa, for her father's job. They moved again for his work, to St. Paul, Minnesota, when Earhart was a junior in high school; then to Springfield, Missouri, for yet another job; and Earhart finally graduated high school in Chicago, where she, her mother, and her sister moved to avoid more of her father's job-related upheaval.

Much of the Midwest at that time was rural, which also meant it was very disconnected from the greater world and new modern conveniences. For example, by the 1930s, while nearly 90 percent of urban homes had electricity, only 10 percent of rural ones did. Earhart always lived in town, so she was lucky enough to have experienced a lot of the innovation occurring at the time.

Atchison was her birthplace, an honor the town still celebrates today, and is the place she lived in the longest during her childhood. It was at its peak when Earhart knew it. It had been one of the first cities in Kansas to have **telegraph** wires; this relatively high-speed form of communication came to Atchison in 1859. Over the years, the town continued to hold a major place in trade and communication. At one point

This mid-1800s Kansas house was Amelia Earhart's first home. It is now a museum dedicated to her.

it served as the headquarters for the US Post Office mailing service to the West. The stagecoach line between it and Placerville, California, was considered a key long-distance route in the country. After the Civil War, the town became an industrial powerhouse, with factories and mills.

Three years after Earhart left, Atchison reached its largest population, 16,500 people. Though it lost its prominence in the country, it still has twenty sites on the National Register of Historic Places and five museums, with special attention paid to Earhart's legacy.

standard as a high school one. New technology means we're living a reality that until recently would have been considered **science fiction**. Yet in many ways, at the turn of the twentieth century, women did not know they could shoot for the stars—or even that there were stars to shoot for.

The Wright Brothers Were Not Always Considered Heroes

Today, the Wright brothers are famous and renowned for achieving flight, but when they first started out they were considered nobodies, and maybe even a bit crazy. Part of this was because of society's lack of understanding and perception of flight. Some of the flying machines looked ridiculous, and not even Earhart herself was impressed the first time she saw one at the Iowa State Fair in 1908, just five years after the Wright brothers' first flight. She described it as "a thing of rusty wire and wood" and said it "looked not at all interesting."

The Wright brothers were the first people to complete a controlled, sustained flight in a human-made aircraft. After their first successful, albeit rough and underpowered, flight in 1903, they spent two years experimenting further. When they finally introduced their work to the world, they had an airplane, the 1905 *Wright Flyer*, which could stay in the air at least half an hour and fly figure eights. Even so, for a long time they could not convince people that the future lay with flight. The US War Department, as well as powerful people in England, France, Germany, and Russia, turned the brothers away in 1905, calling them crazy. Each had heard rumors of flight from others before, and the claims never lived up to the reality. Planes jumped, at most, but could hardly have been said to have flown. Even the first reporter to cover the Wright brothers' work wrote, "Everybody is ready to say, 'Well, what use [is] it? What good will it do?' These are questions no man can answer yet."

Some of the international movers and shakers the Wrights approached thought that they themselves could build their own successful planes. After all, the brothers were "just" bicycle mechanics. Some people reasoned that if the Wright brothers could do it, then one need not be a genius to build a working airplane. These detractors apparently didn't stop to consider that people had been dreaming of flying since at least the ninth century, more than a thousand years earlier, and actively attempting flight since the fifteenth century. Clearly, the Wright brothers were special in order to succeed.

Flying not only took brains but also finances. For their work, the Wright brothers spent about $1,000 on airplane research and development, including travel and shelter, before they finally flew in 1903. That is roughly $70,000 in today's currency—in other words, a lot of money for two bicycle mechanics.

Perhaps part of the reason that people didn't understand just how much was becoming possible in the world was that the Wright brothers' flight was barely covered in the media at the time. The Wright brothers also had lackluster popularity because they abhorred the media. Public opinion about aviation was changing by the time Earhart flew, but Earhart also made good use of the spotlight, unlike the Wright brothers, furthering her cause to bring women into aviation and bring aviation to the masses. The men were both shy and protective of their invention. They did not invite any reporters to their first flights. It wasn't until March 1, 1904, that any press discussed their historic flights. Additionally, that media was not a major newspaper of the day but rather the *Gleanings in Bee Culture*, a beekeeping journal.

The Difference Between Darling and Notorious

If Earhart was "America's darling," then British-born Kenyan Beryl Markham was the world's "notorious woman." At least, this is how Paula McLain, who fictionalized Markham's life for her novel *Circling the Sun*, explains why Markham never became a household name like Earhart did. Markham, five years younger than Earhart, was another impressive **aviatrix** and author of the time, yet few today know her name.

It's true that Earhart was a pioneer, but she did follow some social conventions. For example, she married only once. In contrast, when Markham died at eighty-three, she had been kicked out of school for bad behavior; been married three times and had many affairs; left her son to be raised by his paternal grandmother; and spent time with the Happy Valley set, a group of Europeans who lived in Kenya and were known for their self-indulgence, drug use, and promiscuous lifestyle. Her many professional accomplishments are no less than Earhart's, but because Markham's personality and choices were considered unladylike, she never quite achieved fame.

One of Markham's most famous fans, Ernest Hemingway, is himself well remembered and well regarded for his work, even though he also led a wild life. Hemingway praised Markham's writing. Of her memoir, *West with the Night*, which was published in 1942, five years after Earhart's disappearance, he wrote, "This girl … can write rings around all of us who consider ourselves as writers." The book was reissued nearly forty years after it went

In 1936, Beryl Markham became the first woman to fly solo and nonstop across the Atlantic Ocean from east to west.

out of print, providing Markham some much-needed income in her final three years of life.

Perhaps Markham's most interesting achievement in the history of aviation was her own solo flight across the Atlantic. In 1932, Earhart became the first woman to fly solo nonstop across the Atlantic, traveling from Newfoundland, Canada, to Northern Ireland. Four years later, in 1936, Markham became the first person to fly solo nonstop across the Atlantic east to west, from Britain to Nova Scotia, Canada. Interestingly, where Earhart was widely celebrated and awarded, Markham received moderate reception. Earhart received the Cross of Knight of the Legion of Honor from France, the Distinguished Flying Cross from Congress and the Gold Medal of the National Geographic Society from the United States, and parades. Markham, in contrast, received no such honors, though she did get a ticker-tape parade in New York City.

In that March issue, A. I. Root mentioned the brothers' work deep in his journal, on page 241, to be exact, with one solitary sentence. In September, he covered the Wrights in more detail. In *Gleanings*, an article on flying was a fun aside, and not the main news, as we might now consider it. The Wright brothers' success was buried among articles on "How I Manage Swarming" and "Judging Honey at Fairs." Earhart was among many who would likely not have read such a journal.

Women Had More Than Gravity to Overcome

Learning to fly was not the only obstacle Earhart faced in the pursuit of her career. The tricky mechanics involved in getting early planes off the ground was just one of the things standing in a woman's way at that time. Anita "Neta" Snook, the woman who would later become Earhart's first flight instructor, understood those challenges. Around 1917, Snook applied to the Curtiss Flying School in the town of Newport News, Virginia, because it looked like the best place to study. It was founded by Glenn Curtiss, an aviation pioneer, and was part of the Atlantic Coast Aeronautical Station. The reply to her application was short but definitely not sweet. "No females allowed," it read. How could women be expected to compete in a career when they weren't even allowed to study the field?

Bessie Coleman was another pioneer who faced stiff challenges. Not only was she trying to work outside the home at a time when most women didn't do that, but also her aspirations were in a wild new field that was considered a man's profession. Even more radical, she was also African American and Native American. In the early 1920s, when she sought her pilot's license, the United States legally and socially supported racial discrimination. No flying school in the country

Katherine Sui Fun Cheung was the first Chinese woman to obtain an international flying license, in 1935.

would take Coleman, and other pilots refused to instruct her.

Earhart may not have known of a lot of female pilots before she started in the industry in 1920. There were not many working that she could have known; surely there were fewer than one hundred at the time Earhart bought her first plane. She did appreciate the few female role models she knew of in other male-dominated fields, such as film direction and production, law, advertising, management, and mechanical engineering. She kept a scrapbook of newspaper clippings about these successful women. Ultimately, it wasn't the advice of a person that turned her toward flying. It was a plane. When she was about twenty years old, she and a friend attended a **stunt flying** exposition. One of the planes dove for them to give them a thrill and, more likely, a fright. Earhart stood her ground as the plane approached and then swooped away from her at the last minute. Later she said, "I did not understand it at the time, but I believe that little red airplane said something to me as it swished by."

That something was likely: *Fly.*

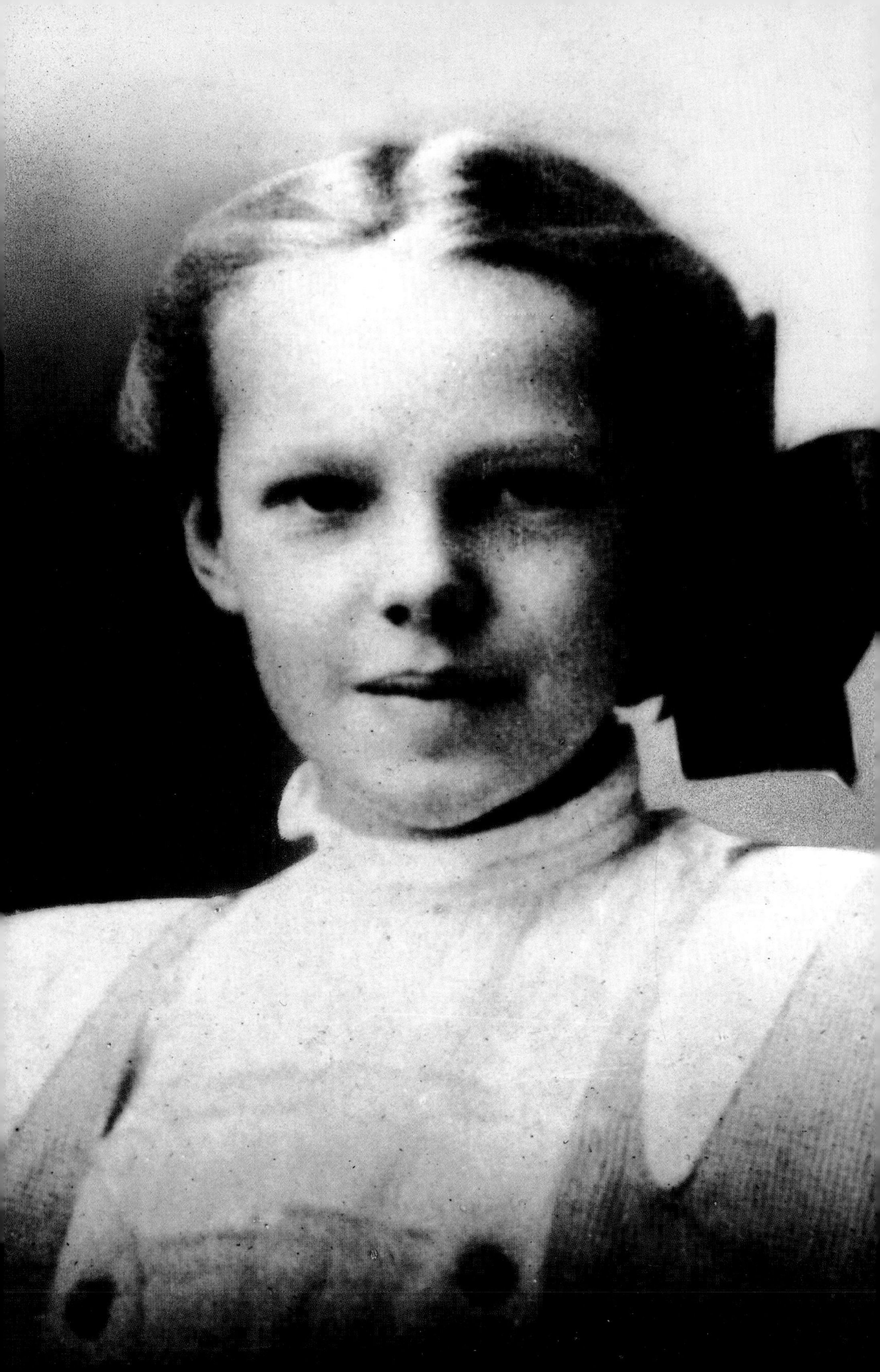

two

Growing Up Curious and Bold

"Better do a good deed near at home than go far away to burn incense."
—Amelia Earhart

Earhart was always on the go during her childhood. She was a curious, active child who earned her grandmother's disapproval. Earhart was outside whenever possible, playing imaginary games and real sports, climbing trees, and in general not acting very much like a lady, in her grandmother's opinion. She was also on the move in that she frequently transferred schools—during one four-year period, she would attend six schools—because of her parents.

Opposite: Young Amelia Earhart never would have guessed she would grow up to be a pilot.

Earhart in Atchison

Named after her two grandmothers, a family tradition, Amelia Mary Earhart was the older of two daughters born to Amelia "Amy" and Samuel "Edwin" Stanton Earhart. She was born July 24, 1897, in Atchison, Kansas, and her sister, Grace Muriel Earhart, came along in 1899. It was good fortune that they had each other as best friends since childhood for them would be a little bit of a roller coaster.

Edwin's career was always in flux. For many years, people might not have realized the reason for his instability, but later, when he could no longer hide his alcoholism from his family or his employers, they would know why life had been so up and down. For a time, Edwin and his wife, Amy, lived in Des Moines, Iowa, while the Earhart sisters lived with their mother's parents in Atchison, attending a private college prep school. Tuition was paid for by Alfred Gideon Otis, the girls' wealthy grandfather, who was a retired US district court judge, president of a bank, and leader in a church.

The two girls seemed to love finding adventure. In Atchison, Millie (or Meelie) and Pidge, as Earhart and her sister were called, spent hours outside, exploring their neighborhood. Earhart earned a reputation as a bold ringleader, followed not just by her little sister but also by her cousins and friends as well.

Glimpses of the Future in a Poem from the Past

Earhart approached school assignments with the same interest and determination that she would later show flying. One such instance that may have left a lasting impression on Earhart was the three weeks she spent memorizing Thomas Babington Macaulay's poem "Horatius" for a speech contest in the seventh grade. Earhart may have been as attracted to the poem's story as she was to the challenge of learning it. We can see aspects of the brave adventurer she would become in the poem's heroes.

First published in 1842, this poem was one of four in Macaulay's book *Lays of Ancient Rome*, which told legends of heroism in early Rome. Poems used to be sung, and Macaulay wrote his in that traditional style. People took to reciting his poems for fun with friends. They were also a popular school memorization exercise, and standard reading well into the 1900s. Winston Churchill, future prime minister of Great Britain, even did so when he was a student. Earhart was thus following a hallowed educational tradition when she took on "Horatius."

The poem tells the story of three heroes who are willing to die in order to prevent the enemy army from crossing the bridge into Rome and likely destroying the city. Macaulay's poem includes some powerful lines that make a reader think also of the hero Earhart would become to many. For example, the poem states: "And how can man die better / Than facing fearful odds." Earhart herself is assumed to have died while daring society's conventions and pushing aeronautics' boundaries—certainly a good death by Macaulay's definition. After a dramatic fight, Horatius ends up having to swim, in his full suit of armor, for the Roman shore. He makes it, and his bravery turns him into a legend: "With weeping and with laughter / Still is the story told, / How well Horatius kept the bridge / In the brave days of old." Still today, eighty-plus years after Earhart's flying days, we study her and applaud her groundbreaking work.

Earhart herself may have had at least a subconscious inkling of her connection to Horatius. Though one of her adventures, mentioned later in this chapter, prevented her from reciting the poem in the contest, she didn't consider her time and energy spent on memorizing it as a waste. "I'm glad to know Horatius anyway," she said, "and it's fun to say it whether I get a prize or not."

Earhart Loved Learning—Even Outside the Classroom

Earhart sometimes ran up against authority at school for speaking her mind, but overall, teachers knew her as a smart student. Many young people today participate in experiential learning, and Earhart may have unintentionally set up some early independent-learning versions of this for herself. In at least two cases, Earhart put her knowledge and creativity to the test in the real world!

Trapped Chickens

Even as a child, Earhart seemed to always focus on finding the solution rather than the problem. She had planted a flower garden in her grandparents' yard. Earhart grew frustrated when a neighbor's chickens started scratching at the dirt and eating the seeds, but rather than give up, she decided to make a trap to catch the stray chickens. Using engineering and construction know-how, which probably included drawing of plans, math, and experimentation, Earhart designed and built a trap from an empty orange crate with a hinged lid to save her garden.

Amelia Earhart's sister, Muriel, also known as Pidge, is pictured here with their mother, Amy.

Earhart's "First Flight"

Another example of Earhart's ingenuity occurred when she was only about seven years old. In an attempt to make her own roller coaster, fashioned after one she saw at the World's Fair in St. Louis, Earhart built a device and took what could be called her first flight. It would be years before she would pursue becoming a pilot; in fact, between this particular event and her first flying lesson, Earhart would scoff at the sight of an actual airplane, as it would appear shabby to her.

In 1904, with the help of her sister, their uncle, and a neighbor boy, Earhart made a ramp out of wooden planks similar in shape to the swoop of a roller coaster. She secured it to the toolshed roof about 8 feet (2.4 meters) high (wonder what her grandmother thought of that!) and then greased the ramp with lard, or animal fat. She constructed a sled out of a broken wooden box and climbed in, volunteering to be the first to try this "roller coaster" out. She slid a little ways and promptly hit the trestle, or side of the ramp, and toppled to the ground. Even though she was a little beat up from the fall and her clothes were torn, she immediately started figuring how to improve upon the design by extending the ramp and straightening the trestle.

"Oh, Pidge," she exclaimed, using her sister's nickname, "it's just like flying!" Today, it's not uncommon for a young child to know what flying feels like, but back then, since neither Earhart nor anyone she'd known had been on a plane, it was like she was telling the future! It was certainly like flying was in her bones, in the very fabric of her being.

Earhart's Character

We can see examples of Earhart's persistent, bold, and considerate nature through the stories of her childhood. Another such account comes from when Earhart was nine. Her father gave her a .22-caliber Hamilton rifle for Christmas. True to her character, Earhart did not use the gun to thoughtlessly shoot animals or even tin-can targets, but to help protect her community, or so she believed.

Earhart was an avid reader, and if she was not outside, she was likely in a library "traveling"—if only by reading about other countries. She had read about the bubonic plague carried by rats where workers were excavating and starting construction on the Panama Canal. She assumed that rats in her hometown of Atchison, Kansas, must also carry the plague. She spent her nights shooting them in her grandparents' barn.

One time, she only wounded the rat, and it managed to drag itself back through its hole in the wall. Perhaps fearing it could still spread disease, and just as likely wanting to leave no wounded animal to suffer, Earhart decided to wait as long as it took for the rat to reappear. An hour later, it did. Unfortunately, her own brand of suffering was soon to begin: her grandparents were so furious at her for being late to dinner that they took her rifle away. Earhart's father said, "She gets an idea in her head, and by golly, she stays right with it. Dinner or no, punishment or not, she wanted to get that rat."

"Neighbor" Bob

As a young woman, Earhart would leave school to volunteer as a nurse during World War I, but that was not the first occasion of Earhart putting life above education, though it was the most dramatic. Years before, when she was still living in Atchison, Kansas, with her sister and grandparents, Earhart paid a needed kindness to a neighbor's horse. On their way to school one day, Earhart and her sister, Muriel, greeted their neighbor Mrs. Colby, who was also one of their grandmother's friends. Mrs. Colby asked the girls to stop by after school to see their friend Bob, her horse. The girls often rode Bob when the Colbys didn't need him for transportation, but that day, Mrs. Colby said that Bob really needed them. The Colbys' in-home helper had had to leave suddenly to help one of his own sick relatives and hadn't tended to Bob before he left. The girls decided that they could stop in quickly before school and return later as well for a longer visit.

They found Bob without food and water, and the carrot and sugar cubes they had in their pockets for him weren't going to be enough until after school. On top of their treats, he needed fresh water, oats, and hay. After they finished helping him, they were late for school and had in fact missed the speech contest Earhart was to participate in by reciting "Horatius." For such a competitive person to miss that event shows her strong understanding of the importance of matters outside the classroom and sacrificing herself for others.

Stand Your Ground

Earhart had the kind of parents who gave a young girl a rifle. It should be no surprise that they also taught her never to run away from a situation. This philosophy came into play when some neighborhood boys in Atchison, Kansas, started to taunt Earhart's dog, James Ferocious. (Not surprising that Earhart would never name a dog Fluffy!) Earhart and her sister adored their dog, who was usually very sweet and lived up to his name only with strangers, as the boys discovered. James Ferocious drove them to climb to the top of a nearby shed for safety.

Hearing him growling and barking from where she was inside the house, Earhart sprang into action. An upset dog can't necessarily distinguish in the moment whom he's scared of or angry at, and by running onto the scene, Earhart was putting herself in danger. Nevertheless, she kept her wits about her and talked to James Ferocious in a firm but kind tone. Once he'd calmed down, she led him into the house, away from his antagonists. When asked later by her mother if she was scared, Earhart replied, "There wasn't any time to be afraid."

Go Big and Don't Go Home

As much as courage, determination, wits, and smarts stayed with Earhart into adulthood, so did her love of exploring and adventure. You can't fly a plane by yourself for weeks at a time without that kind of exuberance. Earhart gravitated toward the extreme at play as a child, and even in her childhood imagination!

She and her sister invented a game called Bogie with their Atchison, Kansas, cousins, Lucy and Kathryn Challis. They took imaginary journeys in an old abandoned carriage, using elaborate maps of a made-up world. In her autobiography, Earhart wrote, "I know I can never be so terrified by anything met with in the real world as by the shadowy play creatures which lurked in the dark corners of the hay mow to attack us, or crept up the creaking steps from the lower stalls." Her sister, Muriel, said that at the end of playing, they were always "hoarse from screaming, damp with perspiration, and streaked with dust and cobwebs, but were always called home just before we reached our imaginary destination—Cherryville."

How poignant that, ultimately, in real life, Earhart also didn't make it to her destination.

Earhart on the Move

In 1908, Earhart and her sister left Atchison to join their parents, moving from Kansas to live and attend school full-time in Iowa. At this point, Edwin had secured a position as claims officer for the Rock Island Railroad, but over the next couple of years, his drinking became an obvious problem, and he lost his job. He checked himself into a month-long treatment. They moved again for work in 1913, to St. Paul, Minnesota, and again, Edwin Earhart could not stay sober. He was lucky that he stayed employed, holding on just barely to a low-level job. That very spring, he was offered a job in Springfield, Missouri. All four of them moved yet again, so soon after their last move. Unfortunately, right after they arrived, they were told there was no job after all. "There are two kinds of stones," Earhart eventually wrote of her father, "one of which rolls." Perhaps this was her resigned acceptance that her father was the other kind of stone.

It was during this same time period that Earhart's grandmother passed away, and the Otis house, Earhart's childhood home, was auctioned, along with all of its contents. With an unstable husband and seemingly no place to go, Amy Earhart decided to leave and moved with her children to Chicago. This was a bold move for a woman at that time. Her husband even told her that if she moved, it would be as though she were abandoning him. She never even tried to encourage her daughters to fit into the era's conventional mold for girls. She now saw she had to do something different in order to do what was best—both for her and for her children.

The Progressive Era and New Opportunities for Women

Earhart was born at the end of an age trapped within social conventions and legalities that benefited the white upper class while exploiting and restricting immigrants, minorities, children, and women. By the 1890s, that grip was starting to loosen. Earhart lived at a true turning point in American civilization. The **Progressive Era**, as it would come to called, lasting from around 1900 to 1929, was certainly a turning point as society started to look forward.

The Progressive Era began as desire for social reform, impacting everything from education to medicine, from the farm to the urban workplace. Women started to win new experiences. In 1870, approximately one-fifth of college and university students were women. Thirty years later, at the dawn of the Progressive Era, that amount had increased to more than one-third. Only 19 percent of all undergraduate degrees went to women, meaning many dropped out before completion, likely to get married or maybe to help aging parents. At least more women started college than ever had before in the country's history. At its founding in 1846, the American Medical Association refused membership to women, but by 1915, it allowed them. Women sought females-only medical schools, but by the 1910s, they were allowed into the country's leading ones. Earhart herself was premed at Columbia University in New York City for a few months in 1919.

In 1916, Jeannette Rankin of Montana became the first woman elected to the United States House of Representatives. That was, oddly, before women even had the right to vote nationally. On August 18, 1920, the Nineteenth Amendment

The Aviation Pioneer Who Taught Earhart

Anita "Neta" Snook was born to be in the air, though she always kept her head out of the clouds. She first experienced the exhilaration of flying from the passenger seat of the family doctor's Ford Model T. A curious child, she'd ride with him on his calls to farms around rural Illinois, and they'd play a game they called flying: he'd race the car to the top of each hill and then speed down the other side.

As much as Snook loved that weightless rush, she was also well grounded. For her, playtime was exploring mechanics and engineering. In 1905, when she was nine, her dad bought a used car, and together they took it apart and reassembled it. She combined these two facets of her personality in order to succeed as one of the first female aviators—she had to have both guts and smarts to find work in the "man's world" of flight. For example, **barnstorming** was a popular job for pilots at that time, so Snook found work in that. Unfortunately, her pilot's license specified the number of passengers she could carry in her plane as "none." Snook erased the *n* so she could carry "one."

Then, in 1920, Snook met the person she would influence the most before her death at age ninety-five (outside of, perhaps, her son, two grandchildren, nine great-grandchildren, and one great-great-grandchild). She became Amelia Earhart's flight instructor. She recognized that although being Earhart's

Standing on the right in this 1922 photo is Neta Snook, Amelia Earhart's first flight instructor.

teacher was only one of her many accomplishments in life, it was the one most people would view as most important. Snook even titled her autobiography, which was about Snook's own life, *I Taught Amelia to Fly*, putting the focus on her famous student.

Snook retired from flying in 1922, at only age twenty-six, as the first woman to have been accepted into flight school, run an aviation company, and run a commercial airfield. She continued to lecture on her and Earhart's careers for decades to come. In 1992, a year after her death, she was inducted into the Iowa Aviation Hall of Fame.

Alice Paul (*top*) and other suffragists celebrate the ratification of the Nineteenth Amendment in 1920.

to the United States Constitution made law of the land that women had all rights and responsibilities, the same as men did, including that they could vote. They did so for the first time on Election Day in November of that year. Reformers and **women's suffrage** advocates, from Elizabeth Cady Stanton to Susan B. Anthony, fought long and hard for this right.

By the start of the twentieth century, 18.8 percent of American women worked outside the home. Though the ability to work was great, the treatment of women by employers and the conditions under which many of them worked were not. Still, even that led to something progressive: the Women's Trade Union League started in 1903, and the US Department of Labor's Women's Bureau started in 1920.

Overlooked by Progress

Improvements of the Progressive Era were rarely 100 percent open minded, and often steps forward were taken only in certain situations. Some things that occurred in this time were downright ugly. For example, **Jim Crow laws** existed throughout the period. Jim Crow laws were enacted in the South after the Civil War. These state and local regulations enforcing racial segregation and discrimination continued through the mid-1960s. In general, African Americans were overlooked throughout the reforms of the Progressive Era.

Still, as a white person from a fairly economically stable background, Earhart was in a position to reap the benefits of this point in American history.

Looking Ahead ... to Earhart's Greatest Adventure and Lasting Legacy

Amelia Earhart is of course so much more than the folklore that surrounds her death, but it is the mystery of her final moments that first introduces so many people to her story. People can't help but wonder: *What really happened to Earhart, her navigator, and her plane? Do the clues and our assumptions really point us toward the truth, or did something unexpected happen?* For most people, this thrilling puzzle makes for interesting conversation among friends, but writer Jane Mendelsohn took her curiosity to another level.

Mendelsohn wrote a novel about Earhart called *I Was Amelia Earhart*, published in 1996. It is a fictional imagining of Earhart's final days on an uninhabited desert island in the middle of the Atlantic Ocean. So many people have speculated about Earhart, and this book speaks to that very human desire to understand the unknown and create myths. The book is written in the first person, as though Earhart is telling her own story, so it also humanizes her, changing her from an icon back into a person. By writing about the accessible side of a very courageous explorer, Mendelsohn was able to see her own bravery just starting out in the world as an adult and writing her first novel.

I Was Amelia Earhart was a finalist for the Orange Prize (now known as the Baileys Women's Prize for Fiction), an award which itself celebrates achievements by women, specifically by honoring the best in writing by women.

Earhart's High School Years

When Earhart arrived in Chicago, she really displayed her devotion to learning and satisfying her curiosity. She refused to attend the school in the district into which her mother moved them because the chemistry lab was below her standards. She researched other options and settled on Hyde Park High School, which was in another part of Chicago. Once again, the family moved.

Also once again, Earhart demonstrated her independence and bold determination to get what she desired. Barely two weeks into the term at Hyde Park, Earhart realized her teachers were horrible. Her English teacher was particularly lacking in ability. Earhart tried to improve the situation by circulating a petition among the students, demanding a more skilled instructor, but the other students didn't care about the ease with which they passed their days. So, Earhart got permission to spend that class period in the library, where she read four times the number of books she would have read had she followed the syllabus.

In June 1916, Earhart graduated from Hyde Park. From then until 1918, she attended Ogontz School, a finishing school near Philadelphia, Pennsylvania, meant to further prepare young women for the world. Fortunately, this one's purpose was more than just grooming its students for domestic life. Headmistress Abby Sutherland wrote to Earhart's mother that she was "very brilliant" and later wrote to George Putnam, who would become Earhart's husband, that she "was always pushing into unknown seas in her reading."

Recruitment posters like this one encouraged people to join the Voluntary Aid Detachment during World War I.

Life Is More than School

Earhart would not graduate Ogontz because World War I interrupted her studies. She was moved by the effects of war, which she saw when she spent Christmas 1917 with her sister, Muriel, in Toronto, Canada, where Muriel herself was busy with school. Earhart volunteered to become involved because she could not stand to spend her time in the classroom while people were dying on the battlefield. The United States was brand new to the war, so Earhart had not seen its effects in Pennsylvania, but Canada, a dominion of the British Empire, had been fighting in it for over three years, since August 4, 1914. When Earhart was in Toronto, injured Canadian soldiers were arriving home, and Earhart got a shocking look at the damage war does.

Though school was important to Earhart, she had a strong sense of priorities that put life, and her fellow living creatures, first. She left Ogontz early the next year, and after training as a nurse's aid with the Red Cross, joined the VAD, the Voluntary Aid Detachment, in Toronto. A lot of her work was nontechnical, since she didn't have a degree. She cleaned, served meals, and entertained patients, but she did put in some time in the pharmacy. She had taken a lot of chemistry classes and done well in all her lab work. She served in this way for nearly a year, till November of 1918, when the armistice, the agreement to stop fighting, was signed.

three

Her Journey and Final Adventure

"When a great adventure's offered you, you don't refuse it, that's all."
—Amelia Earhart

In 1918, Earhart's volunteer duties had her nursing during night shifts at the Spadina Military Hospital. Unfortunately, during this time the Spanish flu had also reached Toronto, and Earhart, along with many others, fell ill. She suffered from pneumonia, followed by operations on her sinuses, and was sick for almost a year. In fact, Earhart would have issues with

Opposite: Amelia Earhart (*right*) stands beside her first airplane, a Kinner Airster, with her instructor, Neta Snook.

her sinuses throughout her life. By this time, her sister was living in Massachusetts, and Earhart went to stay with her and recover.

Inspired by her nursing experience, Earhart enrolled in Columbia University's premed program and started class in the fall of 1919. She lasted a year there. Despite her good grades, she realized she didn't want to be a doctor. She was interested in medicine but not in the day-to-day tasks of a practicing physician. She also hadn't started school on the best foot because she was still not entirely well. In addition, her parents were back together, trying again to make their marriage work, and living in Southern California. Earhart allowed herself to be tempted to move back in with them. It seemed, for many reasons, like the right time to be with them and regroup about what she wanted to do.

Her Passion Awakens

If the time between World War I and World War II was the golden age of aviation, so called for its exciting innovation, promise, and celebrity, then Southern California was the diamond on the gold ring. With climate perfect for year-round flying, the area was a hub of activity. One of the first commercial passenger jets, the DC-1, would be produced there in 1933.

On December 28, 1920, Earhart's dad took her to an air show and arranged for her to ride along on a "trial hop," or take off and land. Immediately, Earhart was hooked, and her passion for flight flourished. As she said, "By the time I had got two or three hundred feet off the ground, I knew I had to fly." Not even a week later, on January 3, 1921, Neta Snook gave

Earhart her first flying lesson. "I liked her on sight," Snook wrote in her autobiography, *I Taught Amelia to Fly*.

After six months, Earhart set her sights on buying one of the Kinner Airsters. They were designed and built by Winfield "Bert" Kinner, who owned the airfield where Earhart was learning to fly. Snook had arranged to test-fly his planes in exchange for use of his airfield for her business flying tours and teaching pilots, so Snook knew the planes, and she discouraged Earhart from buying. She found the Airsters underpowered, tippy, and unreliable. Earhart liked the planes for the positive side of that equation: the simple cooling system meant there was less to worry about, and the light weight meant she could move one of the planes by its tail under her own power—no dolly and no man needed for help. Snook may have been eventually proved right. After only a couple of years owning her first Kinner Airster, which she called the *Canary*, Earhart sold it. Immediately, its new owner took it for a flight and crashed it, killing himself and his passenger.

Earhart's mother had given her enough to cover the plane's price, $2,000, and Earhart picked up and subsequently dropped a series of odd jobs to help with expenses: phone company clerk, photographer, file clerk, truck driver, and gravel hauler. It was in the bright-yellow-painted *Canary* that Earhart passed her flying license tests on December 15, 1921. Less than a year later, in October 1922, she set her first flying record: she got the plane to 14,000 feet (4,267 m). On May 16, 1923, the Fédération Aéronautique Internationale (FAI) made her the sixteenth woman to earn its international pilot's license. Technically, with that license, she could officially set flight records; however, curiously, the FAI did not recognize records made by women until 1928.

The Birth of a Media Darling

By the time she had her license, Earhart had already started to earn her media chops. Her first crash, the previous summer, in 1921, ended up being a media affair. That was because anything related to air travel made the news in those days. Snook reported that mechanical error caused the issue: the Kinner Airster's third cylinder was always clogging with oil. She also reported that she would have done exactly as Earhart had to try to save the flight. When all was known to be lost, Earhart had the presence of mind to stay calm and crash well, handling everything right. So calm was Earhart's demeanor that humorously, when Snook looked over at her seconds after the crash, she saw Earhart powdering her nose in preparation for the reporters.

A year later, in the summer of 1922, the *Los Angeles Examiner* quoted Earhart as saying that she would like to fly across the continent.

Earhart's First Big Break

Earhart had exhibited hints of her father's instability before, but after 1924 she really started bouncing around. First, she ended up back in the hospital because of her lungs. Then, when she sold the *Canary*, she moved back east, driving across the country with her mother because her parents had split again. She lasted not quite a year at Columbia University, and then she joined her mother and sister in Boston. She tried to start another academic program, taking a class at Harvard in 1926 and applying to the Massachusetts Institute of Technology (MIT). She also had a habit of starting and quitting jobs. Then, in the spring of 1928, while she was working as a counselor in a vocational-guidance service for women, tutoring Syrian and Chinese immigrants in English, Earhart got the first big opportunity of her flying career.

The gossip among the higher-ups in the aviation world was that the then popular, and still today famous, explorer Richard E. Byrd had sold one of his planes. The trimotored Fokker went to a wealthy woman who wasn't a pilot but who wanted to be the first woman to fly, or rather be a passenger on a flight, across the Atlantic. Many were inspired by Charles Lindbergh, the aviator who made the first nonstop solo flight from New York to Paris across the Atlantic in 1927, and Mrs. Amy Guest was no exception. It was that kind of time: the wealthy were buying experiences. Interestingly, Captain Hilton H. Railey would get this information from George Putnam, the man who would go on to become Earhart's husband.

Guest was the wife of the former British secretary of state for air. Her family was worried about this flight of fancy she had planned, and they asked Railey to help them find someone with the right image to sit in her place. If Guest was happy with her alternate, she would likely acquiesce, they believed. Railey spoke with an acquaintance in the Boston chapter of the National Aeronautic Association, who directed him to call Earhart at work. She had joined the association in 1927, and her name showed up in the media here and there; she became known as an advocate for aviation and female pilots.

As unlikely as it seems, at first Earhart dismissed his call. "I'm too busy to answer just now," she said that afternoon. Yet the fates seemed to intervene, and Railey persisted. The world would have been different if he had not. Earhart eventually took the call, and later that day she visited Railey in his office. "How would you like to be the first woman to fly the Atlantic?" Railey said to her. He later recalled, "Only a flicker in her cool eyes betrayed the excitement this question must have aroused."

This was the conversation during which Earhart received the nickname Lady Lindy. As Railey watched her talk about her experience to date, and her lack of it, including that she could not fly with instruments alone and had few flight hours with trimotored aircraft, he decided that she looked like the celebrated young Lucky Lindy, Charles Lindbergh. Lindbergh was a media sensation following his flight on May 20–21, 1927, and indeed had achieved a place in history as well. Guest "had stipulated that the person to whom she would yield must be 'representative' of American women," Railey wrote. "In Amelia Earhart I felt that I had discovered not their norm but their sublimation."

All the pieces had to have fallen into place for Earhart to have gotten this opportunity, which would lead to so much more. Even still, not everyone was in support of the journey. Railey's wife urged Earhart to reconsider; the whole trip made her uneasy. In reply, Earhart said, "When a great adventure's offered you, you don't refuse it, that's all."

The Voyage of the Friendship

On June 17, 1928, Earhart left Newfoundland as a passenger in the *Friendship*, with Wilmer Stultz piloting and Louis Gordon copiloting. They arrived in Wales less than a full day later, on June 18. The crowd gathered there went wild. Though Earhart felt she had been "just baggage, like a sack of potatoes," there was no denying she'd been the first female on a plane across the Atlantic. Upon returning to the United States, the three were greeted with a ticker-tape parade in New York City, and Earhart's celebrity blossomed.

Putnam stepped forward again, this time to help Earhart write a book, what would be called *20 Hrs. 40 Min., Our Flight in the Friendship: The American Girl, First Across the Atlantic by Air, Tells Her Story*. She lived at Putnam's house, along with him and his then wife, while they worked on the book.

Piloting Her Love Life

Earhart may not have been in charge on her first superstar flight, but she was in charge from then on, both in the air and on the ground, whether in her aviation pursuits or her romantic adventures. Putnam would not be the first, and certainly not the last, person she would have a major affair with. She piloted each relationship.

Her first long-lasting relationship started years before her involvement with Putnam, but continued to linger, and the associations did overlap. Earhart met Samuel Chapman when he was a boarder in her parents' home before their final breakup. Chapman and Earhart got along very well. Both of them considered marriage to be an equal partnership, which was progressive for the times. She agreed to marry him but never did. They stayed loosely together, living apart, for six years.

When Putnam interviewed Earhart during the *Friendship* flight arrangements, he was married. What's more, Earhart and his wife, Dorothy Binney Putnam, became friends. Earhart even wanted to dedicate her book to her. In 1929, Putnam and his wife divorced, and it would take six proposals from Putnam before Earhart said yes. They would finally marry on February 7, 1931. Her yes carried conditions, which included her keeping

Amelia Earhart and her husband, George Palmer Putnam, pose together for a photo.

her “flying name” and not taking his last name as hers. She made the rest of her needs clear in a letter to him right before their wedding.

“You must know again my reluctance to marry, my feeling that I shatter thereby chances in work which means most to me,” Earhart wrote to Putnam in her letter. She went on to say that though she knew there would be beautiful things about the union, it was hard for her to imagine them right then when all she could think of was the risk this posed for her career.

She asked for space, both literal and metaphorical, desiring that they not spend every moment together or get too much into the other’s business or pleasure. She also maintained that they could, and should, expect each other to have relationships outside the marriage. “I shall not hold you to any midaevil [sic] code of faithfulness to me nor shall I consider myself bound to you similarly.”

Earhart closed this prenuptial letter as sweetly as she seemed able: “I will try to do my best in every way and give you that part of me you know and seem to want.” Ever practical, Earhart also issued one final condition: “Let me go in a year if we find no happiness together.”

It is expected that, as a legendary figure, Earhart and her personal life would be the subject of rumors and speculation. Some think there is proof of an affair Earhart had with Eugene Vidal due to entries to that effect in Earhart’s secretary’s diary and speculations by Vidal’s family. Vidal did spend a lot of time at the Putnams’ home and eventually became a business partner of Earhart’s; he was a pilot himself, as well as an airline executive. Perhaps the biggest evidence of an affair was that Earhart likely got him his most high-profile job, and later saved him from being fired from it.

Earhart was friends with Franklin and Eleanor Roosevelt when they were in the White House, and the president made Vidal the director of the Bureau of Air Commerce. Vidal was let go in 1936 when the bureau was reorganized. In response, Earhart wrote a "breathtakingly cheeky" letter to First Lady Roosevelt, threatening to not campaign for her husband's reelection. The next day, Vidal was back to work. This certainly suggests that, romantic affair or not, Earhart was in the pilot's seat of her relationship with Vidal, and maybe of her relationship with the First Family of the United States!

Earhart the Star

Putnam's promise that Earhart would become a celebrity after her first **transatlantic** flight and book were fulfilled. With her fame, Earhart got endorsements from products like Lucky Strike cigarettes; in 1928 and 1929, her image appeared in print ads. The ads claimed Earhart had chain-smoked during her whole first transatlantic trip in order to keep her stress from being a passenger low. However, the screenwriters of the 2009 movie *Amelia* claim that their research revealed that Earhart didn't smoke. It could also be argued that she hardly seemed to be the kind of person who got stressed out, certainly not by being a passenger. Indeed, she would go on to set speed and distance records, and some theorize that during her final flight she even successfully landed a failing aircraft on a tiny island in the middle of the Pacific Ocean.

Building on her fame, Earhart announced her own fashion line, Amelia Earhart Fashion. Since her style already garnered media attention, she promoted her clothes as functional for "active living." It got a lot of press yet did not maintain popularity, and unfortunately did not net the profit Earhart had hoped. The line launched in late 1933 and folded before Earhart's disappearance in 1937. Between flying and her other endeavors, perhaps Earhart could not devote enough time to the business, but likely being in the middle of the Great Depression caused a lack in sales.

Earhart started a national lecture tour for her first book and her second, *The Fun of It*, published in 1932. In 1935, one of her speeches, connecting women to science, was broadcast over the radio, so lots of people heard it. Of course, lots of people were hearing her in person: Putnam put her on an intense presentation schedule, at one point booking her for twenty-nine lectures in thirty-one days.

Earhart the Advocate

Earhart became aviation editor for *Cosmopolitan* magazine, serving in this capacity from 1928 to 1930. She published sixteen articles with them, using her position to promote women in aeronautics. "Shall You Let Your Daughter Fly?" and "Why Are Women Afraid to Fly?" were two of her articles. At the time, even flying as a passenger on a commercial flight was exotic, and done way more by men than by women. Earhart wrote about both her adventures and the importance of flying becoming more commonplace for everyone. Her words clashed with other opinions being printed. A year before Earhart accepted the *Cosmo* assignment, *Liberty* magazine printed the woman-penned "Why I Believe Woman Pilots Can't Fly the Atlantic."

All of the endorsements and projects enabled Earhart to continue to fly. It was a good thing that she did spend most of her time flying, or she might have appeared to become less of a practicing aviator and more of a brand, as we might call her today. Earhart was, in fact, worried about that. People started to talk: rumor was spreading that she was just a star, and that her publicist husband was using promotions to mask her lack of competence as a pilot. Never one to roll over under the pressure of idle gossip, Earhart kept making her own self-powered waves.

"Ships and Spirits Tuned in Rhyme"

On November 2, 1929, Earhart cofounded the Ninety-Nines, the first organization for women aviators. All of the women pilots who existed at the time, all 117 of them, were invited to join. Ninety-nine women would form the charter membership, and that was what would inspire the group's name. The group would offer mutual support, and the members would work toward the advancement of aviation. Additionally, there would be record keeping for women in flight, with a central office to keep files. Cofounder Louise Thaden was the first elected official as secretary, and was instrumental in keeping the group together.

In 1941, Dick Ballou's "Song of the Ninety-Nines" became of the group's official song:

> In the air, everywhere,
> It's the song of The Ninety-Nines.
> Wings in flight,
> Day and night,
> With the Song of The Ninety-Nines.
> On the line,
> Fliers fine,
> Ships and spirits tuned in rhyme,
> Keep that formation

Over the nation
With the song of The Ninety-Nines.

Equal Rights

As long as Earhart had been flying, she'd been championing women's rights. It could be argued she had been as long as she had been alive. Even when she was playing sports as a young person, she was asking for support for girls and women in activities equal to that of boys and men. It was no surprise, then, that she was an outspoken supporter of the Equal Rights Amendment. She met with President Herbert Hoover on September 22, 1932, to urge passage of the amendment. National Woman's Party members Burnita Matthews, Anna Kelton Wiley, and Ruth Taunton attended the meeting with her. She said, "I know from practical experience of the discriminations which confront women when they enter an occupation where men have priority in opportunity, advancement and protection ... I feel that similar equality should be carried into all fields of endeavor, so that men and women may achieve without handicap because of sex."

She was also happy to join the Purdue University staff as a women's career counselor and advisor in aeronautics in 1935. She got the job after speaking there in 1934, by invitation of the university president. She would be a featured speaker there once again, in December 1935, at Purdue's Conference on Women's Work and Opportunities.

No Longer a "Sack of Potatoes"

Between cofounding the Ninety-Nines in 1929 and becoming the organization's first president in 1931, Earhart set the women's speed record: 181.18 miles (291.58 kilometers) per hour, on July 5, 1930. Before her final flight, many more records were to come, in quick succession. If Putnam was running her on overdrive with lectures, Earhart was putting herself through the wringer checking off landmark feats in the air.

Her records included one for altitude and one for distance in 1933, flying across the United States and back in an autogiro, an early aircraft, and breaking her own transcontinental speed record. On January 11, 1935, she was the first person to fly solo the 2,408 miles (3,875 km) from Honolulu, Hawaii, to Oakland, California. Later she reflected on warming up with a thermos of hot chocolate as she flew: "That was the most interesting cup of chocolate I have ever had, sitting up eight thousand feet over the middle of the Pacific Ocean quite alone." She was also the first person to fly solo from Los Angeles to Mexico City (1935); she broke the speed record for a nonstop flight from Los Angeles to Mexico City, and from Mexico City to Newark, New Jersey; and she set the speed record for the fastest east-west crossing from Oakland, California, to Honolulu, Hawaii (1937).

Yet that was not all. She also managed to make good on one of the first oaths she swore: that she would actually take the controls on a flight across the Atlantic. On May 20, 1932, four years after the *Friendship* flew, Earhart launched a single-engine Lockheed Electra from Newfoundland, Canada, where the *Friendship* had departed from as well. The trip was planned to occur exactly five years after Lindbergh made a similar solo journey to become the first man to fly across the ocean. On May 21, Earhart landed, successfully, in Northern Ireland, becoming the first aviatrix to complete the flight alone.

She certainly was no "sack of potatoes" this time, as she lamented she had been on her previous transatlantic flight. Her accolades were many: Earhart received the Distinguished Flying Cross from Congress and the Cross of Knight of the Legion of Honor from the French government. She was the first woman to receive the Gold Medal of the National Geographic Society, which was presented to her by President Hoover. The site of her landing now has a small museum, the Amelia Earhart Centre.

Earhart's Final Adventure

Earhart's work with women at Purdue University helped to finance her biggest glass-ceiling-breaking dream yet: to fly around the world. Though she would not be the first pilot to attempt it, she would be the first to do so along the equator, Earth's widest point, "as near its waistline as could be." She called the Lockheed Electra 10E that she had built for her thirty-ninth birthday a "flying laboratory," but when she requested the special modifications, she had only one journey in mind.

A Small Target to Find

Earhart needed a partner in this venture, specifically, a navigator. The South Pacific was poorly mapped at that time, and even today some consider it "a horizon-to-horizon stretch of unmarked nothing." Ultimately, two navigators were chosen. Harry Manning was a sea captain Earhart met as passenger on his ship back from Europe after her 1928 transatlantic flight. Fred Noonan, the second navigator selected, had also started his career on the water. For twenty years he served as everything from lowly crew member to World War I sailor to master of

This map shows how small and far apart the islands along Amelia Earhart's last flight were, making landing difficult.

steamships. At age forty-four, he moved from water to air and ended up creating the Manila Clipper transpacific route for Pan American Airways.

The US Commerce Department's under-construction emergency landing strip and weather station on Howland Island was determined to be the best place for Earhart to refuel during the Pacific leg of the trip. A US Coast Guard ship, the *Itasca*, would be nearby. Noonan was to navigate from Hawaii to Howland, and the *Itasca* crew would help Earhart land on the island. Still, that was hardly an ideal option, and Earhart knew it.

In planning the 1935 Pacific flight, Earhart chose flying from Hawaii to California, rather than in the reverse direction, because, as she said, "It's easier to hit a continent than an island." However, Howland Island is incredibly small, 0.5 miles wide and 2 miles long (0.8 km by 3.22 km), and perhaps scariest, it rises only 18 feet (5.5 m) above sea level. It would actually be quite easy to misplace this small patch of land.

It's also hard to be perfectly precise all the time, especially over a vast ocean of mostly empty blue, and timing would be crucial for Earhart to connect with the *Itasca*. Sir Gordon Taylor, who himself made early flights across the Pacific and surveyed air transport routes for the Allies in World War II, discussed in his autobiography the difficulty of landing on an island. He was an expert, and one time he reached Hawaii with only five minutes of fuel left.

Even the two expert pilots Earhart made her famous first transatlantic flight with miscalculated their location on that voyage. She had felt down about her lack of experience relative to theirs, but Gordon and Stultz weren't infallible superstars. They missed a much bigger island than Howland. They were supposed to have flown from Canada to Ireland, but set down near neighboring Wales instead. Unpredictable weather knocked their radio useless and obscured their vision. In the fog and rain, even with instruments, they were no longer sure where they were. Eventually forced to land in the water because they were dangerously low on fuel, they learned they were off the shore of the wrong country.

The First Attempt

Earhart made her first attempt, along with the small crew she'd assembled, which included not only two navigators, but also an advisor. Paul Mantz, a Hollywood stunt pilot who had been tutoring Earhart in long-distance flying and navigation, would serve as her technical advisor. On March 17, 1937, the four departed from Oakland, California, for Hawaii.

They experienced some technical problems and ended up laying over in Honolulu for three days while the plane was fixed. When they went to leave, they got no farther than the runway. A tire blew, said several witnesses, or there was pilot error, said Mantz. Either way, while no human suffered harm, the plane was too damaged for quick repairs to correct. The flight was scrapped.

Forty-Two Days of Flying

Owing to Manning's previous commitments and, a rumored contract dispute with Mantz, Earhart and Noonan would be the only crew on the next attempt. Earhart's husband and a mechanic joined them for the Oakland to Miami leg. The second trip officially started on June 1, 1937.

They flew for forty-two days before they went missing. What a strange experience that must have been: over a month of just flying. The records we have don't mention much of what happened during that time, except what stops were made and for what reason. We do know they had to make a longer-than-necessary stop in Lae, New Guinea, starting June 29, because Earhart came down with dysentery. It took her days to recuperate. Weakened by recent illness, Earhart then climbed back into the cockpit to keep going.

Any out-of-sorts feeling that may have lingered in Earhart is unknown. Of all the theories, no one has blamed sickness-related pilot error. Sadly, whatever the cause of their disappearance, it was likely just as random as her illness, and also perhaps as faultless. Earhart disappeared with Noonan between Lae, New Guinea, and Howland Island on July 2, 1937.

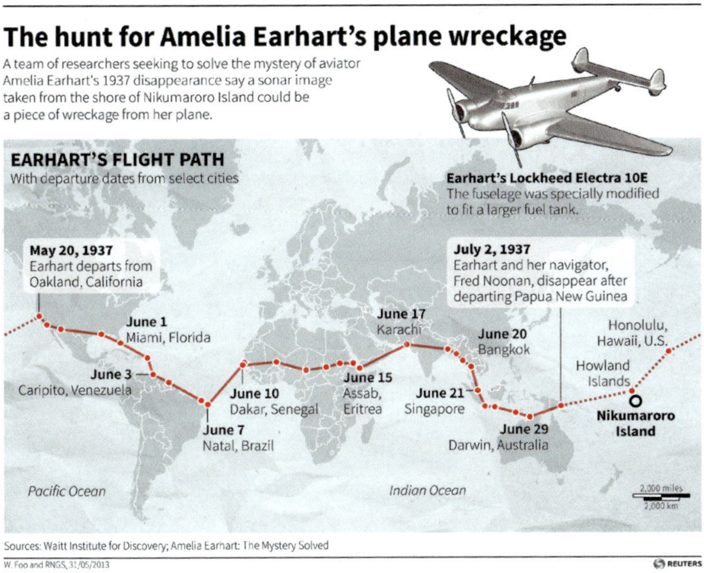

This was Amelia Earhart's last flight path, in 1937.

The Blame Game

For a long time, many people did place blame squarely on both Earhart and Noonan. People assumed she crashed into the ocean after panicking about not being able to find Howland Island, and not being able to reach help by radio. Others also suggested that Noonan was a drunk.

Some did not necessarily blame Earhart, but they also couldn't accept that she died in a relatively expected manner, even though she was a pilot flying a dangerous route in the early days of aviation. A 1943 movie, *Flight for Freedom*, depicts Earhart as an American spy, causing people to wonder if she had in fact been working at the request of her known friend Franklin Roosevelt, president at the time of her death. Although the movie called itself fiction, that did not stop viewers from thinking it presented a probable truth.

In January 2016, W. C. Jameson published his book *Amelia Earhart: Beyond the Grave*, in which he claims to offer proof that Earhart set off across the Pacific Ocean toward one of America's key enemies at the time, Japan. While spying with secret cameras installed in her Lockheed Electra 10E, Earhart was captured by the enemy. The book states that she may have survived World War II. Jameson also presents theories about what could have happened after her supposed capture. She may have died in Japanese custody after capture on the island of Saipan, or perhaps the Japanese released her in 1945. She may have returned to live in the United States as Irene Craigmile Bolam, a banker in New Jersey, until her death of old age in 1982. She may have been Tokyo Rose, broadcasting propaganda and misinformation to American soldiers for the Japanese during World War II.

It is important to note that there are plenty of holes in all of the theories, including a lack of actual physical evidence. In fact, Bolam launched a lawsuit against the first author and publisher that claimed Bolam was Earhart. Furthermore, Tokyo Rose was a persona adopted by a group of English-speaking women, including Iva Toguri d'Aquino. D'Aquino was even convicted of treason in 1949, and eventually pardoned by Gerald Ford on his last day as president, in 1977.

New Perspective and New Understanding

Part of the problem with an unsolved, decades-old mystery is that there has been plenty of time for incorrect, biased speculation to take root. Real people become fictionalized and mythologized. On the other hand, the benefit of time is that over the years, more evidence can come to light, and we can analyze clues with a modern perspective. Over the nearly eighty years since Earhart's fateful flight, there's a lot of new understanding.

Characters Made Real

Although she has passed into myth, we can try to look at Earhart's story objectively. There is evidence that she was a fine pilot; there also is evidence that she had limited experience. There's reason to think flying was a hobby in the midst of so many other aspects of her career, and there's reason to think she kept her eye on the most important prize—working as a full-time pilot—the whole time. What there doesn't seem to be is evidence that she made decisions lightly, especially with another life—such as Noonan's, in this case—in her hands. As a young person, Earhart always seemed to put the needs of others before her own.

Moreover, there also do not seem to be tales of her panicking in any situation, even while in the cockpit. Remember her first instructor's approval of the way Earhart calmly handled her first crash. Snook herself said she would have made the same choices, and she marveled at how Earhart stayed cool even during the post-crash media rush, powdering her nose. During her first transatlantic flight, she coolly helped to problem-solve. Although back then Earhart could not offer any piloting or copiloting expertise, she still stayed focused on finding some other way to help. Desperate to get a read on where they were, Gordon and Stultz detoured toward an oceanliner they spotted in the distance. Earhart wrote a note asking for help, slit open one of the oranges she'd brought along as a snack, stuffed the note inside it, and threw it at the ship.

Her second transatlantic flight, which was her first solo one, was not without failures. Earhart had to have been composed and thoughtful in her choices and well prepared before takeoff in order to survive as she did. Remember also her casual logic when she was a child, choosing not what was expected of her as a girl but what felt most right. She said of her transatlantic solo flight that she placed her trust not in luck but in her mechanic, which was probably good, as luck was not with her on that particular flight.

Only three hours in, her altimeter failed. Earhart quickly switched to using alternative methods to track her altitude, but she was never quite sure exactly how high in the air she was. Four hours in, she ran into a horrible storm. A seam in her exhaust manifold split open. She tried to climb out of the clouds, and then went too high. She could see ice forming on her windshield. Sure enough, the plane started to seize and went into a downward spin. She lost the problem of the ice in the warmer temperatures closer to Earth, but she was also frighteningly low—and spinning. "How long I spun, I do not know. I do know that I did my best to do exactly what one should do with a spinning plane and regained flying control."

Only two hours left to landing and the sound and smell of fuel dripping onto her shoulder told her there was a leak from the cabin fuel gauge. With the growing split in the exhaust manifold, a fire could get easily out of control. Earhart made the sound decision to land. Unfortunately, she was not near her planned landing spot, and she could see no other airfields. She chose the next best thing, a pasture, and after circling it a bit to check her approach, she put down away from the cows. She wrote later, "The actual doing of a dangerous thing, it seems to me, may require little courage. The preparation for it—the acceptance of the inevitable risks involved—may be a far greater test of morale."

More Rumors

It is also unsubstantiated that Fred Noonan was an alcoholic. That theory wasn't proposed until 1966, nearly thirty years later. There was no mention of his drinking at the time of the disappearance, and it would have been talked about if people were worried about that in 1937. Noonan was not a person people would try to protect; in fact, he'd recently divorced, hardly a badge of honor at the time. The scant evidence supporting the alcoholism theory is a police report of a DUI from 1937, but that report has never been found since it was first reported on in 1966, so we don't know if it ever existed. Even if that report were true, it didn't make him an alcoholic. In *Amelia Earhart's Shoes: Is the Mystery Solved?*, Thomas King states, "One can speculate that he drank himself silly once the plane was in the air ... One could also speculate that he had a nervous breakdown, went blind, or was possessed by the devil." In other words, there's no evidence for any of those things, so they're equally as likely or, more probably, equally as unlikely.

Earhart the Island Castaway: A Hypothesis

Interest in solving the mystery has never quite disappeared, although attempts to find the answer once and for all have not been successful. The first search for Earhart, conducted by the Coast Guard and the US Navy by President Roosevelt's orders, was called off just a little over two weeks after Earhart's last transmission. George Putnam privately financed a search as well, but he ended it in October. Both efforts had been unable to find any signs of the Electra. Earhart's death was officially declared in January 1939. However, after all of that, people still couldn't let go of the hunt for Earhart, Noonan, or their plane, and beyond tales of a crash at sea, new signs continue to come to light and suggest a different ending.

Piecing Together Communications Logs

Earhart was to communicate with the *Itasca* on a prearranged schedule, but that didn't happen. Some fault may lie with as frustrating a point as time zones: the *Itasca* was in what could be considered a half time zone, an odd slice of space that differs from other time zones not by an hour, like most, but by half an hour. If Earhart didn't know that, she and the *Itasca* may have been trying to communicate at times when the other party wasn't paying attention.

The International Group for Historic Aircraft Recovery (TIGHAR) investigators think she couldn't hear the *Itasca* even if timing was right. In examining a video clip of Earhart's last takeoff, from Lae, New Guinea, taken by a Guinea Airways employee, TIGHAR believes they found evidence that the communications-receiving antenna had broken during takeoff. Originally in the archives of the Ninety-Nines, the tape came to light when the Experimental Aircraft Association used it in a film about Earhart. Not only does the clip show a "fit and cheerful" Earhart and Noonan, and a takeoff that was "well executed" despite the wind, but it also seems to show the antenna breaking and getting ripped from the plane. The antenna was secured under the plane, not visible to Earhart and Noonan, so it could have easily gone unnoticed. Witnesses on the ground wouldn't have noticed either, unless they'd been looking in just the right place at just the right moment. Even then, they may not have realized what was happening.

At 6:15 a.m. on July 2, 1937, Earhart radioed the *Itasca* for the first known time: she was 200 miles (322 km) from Howland Island. At 100 miles (161 km) out, the *Itasca* let her know that the direction finder couldn't read her location, and they asked her to adjust her settings so they could pinpoint her. There was no reply from Earhart.

At 7:42 a.m., two different *Itasca* radiomen recorded what they heard next from Earhart. "We must be on you but cannot see you … but gas is running low," William Galten reported her saying. Thomas O'Hare recorded, "Only ½ hour gas left sez she."

The ship and the plane continued unsuccessfully to try to pinpoint the other's location. Finally, at 8:43 a.m., Earhart said that they were flying along a line located at "157" southeast and "337" northwest. At 8:55 a.m., she was last heard saying, "We are running north and south."

The search for Earhart began immediately, with the *Itasca* heading off in one direction to look for her and, over the next couple of days, two more ships, the *Colorado* and the *Lexington*, arriving and searching.

Listening to Messages Long After the Crash

Included in the search-and-rescue range was Gardner Island, now called Nikumaroro, 400 miles (644 km) southeast of Howland Island, and a plausible landing place, considering Earhart's direction and gas level. It is a "brutally hot place

A Different Kind of Perspective

Earhart approached religion the way she did other things: with curiosity and an open mind. This was not necessarily the case for others living during her time. The United States is known as a country with religious freedoms, since the very first Protestant settlers who moved here to practice their beliefs in peace. Yet the legal protection of religion does not equate to actual understanding, tolerance, acceptance, and support among the various denominations.

During Earhart's time, the landscape in America was changing. Urban areas were growing. By 1900, fifty US cities were at a population of at least one hundred thousand people. As many as 587 cities had at least ten thousand people—a huge increase in a relatively short amount of time, since by comparison only around 84 cities were that size in 1860. This population growth was in part caused by immigration from other countries. Religious diversity also increased. The first mosques were built in 1915 Maine and 1919 Connecticut. The Red Crescent Society, patterned after the Red Cross but using a symbol commonly associated with Islam, started in Detroit, Michigan, in 1920. Orthodox Judaism became more of an organized force at the turn of the nineteenth century as well.

At the same time, divisions within the sects formed. Presbyterians and Episcopalians in effect divided into separate white and black denominations. Mormons were so formally oppressed in society that they almost dissolved by 1887. In fact, hostility toward the religion would be part of the reason the Utah Territory, where most Mormons lived, did not become a state until 1896. Anti-Semitism swelled starting in the late 1890s, and immigration quotas from the 1920s would remain in effect even during World War II, preventing Jews trying to flee Nazi-controlled countries.

Earhart was baptized in the Episcopal Church as a child, but she didn't stay a practicing Episcopalian. Instead, she relished scientific study of religion, and preferred to satisfy her curiosity and learn about other religions. She was fascinated by the story of food miraculously appearing to Israelites during their forty years in the desert after they left Egypt. She tried to bake her own manna, a kind of angel food cake popover, repeatedly experimenting with recipes of her own creation.

As an adult, Earhart enjoyed talking with others about world religions. She tried to get her flight instructor, Neta Snook, to join her in reading the Quran. Snook refused on the grounds that there was no mention of Muhammad, the founder of Islam, in the Bible. Earhart respected the viewpoints of others, and the same could be said of Snook since rather than the disagreements and violence that can happen around talk of religion, the two women approached their different perspectives without anger.

inhabited by foot-long centipedes and giant carnivorous crabs." TIGHAR investigators believe Earhart landed there and sent radio signals out nightly for five nights. They claim to know of a hundred messages from Earhart, minus some hoaxes, that reached shortwave radio users as far as Florida, which would be a possible occurrence under the right conditions.

Betty Klenck was as teenager in Florida when she heard a voice on her family's shortwave radio: "This is Amelia Earhart. Help me!" She recorded what she could hear, including what sounded like "a woman crying, calling for help and arguing with a man who seemed to be delirious." There was, however, no sign of Earhart, Noonan, or the plane when US Navy ships passed by the island. Perhaps the downed plane got swept away in a storm before the navy got near the island. Maybe Earhart and Noonan were on a different part of the island when the rescuers came by. Earhart did report in an early message that Noonan was injured, so he may have died soon after landing.

Finding Meaning in Ocean Garbage

Since the 1980s, TIGHAR has been collecting evidence and leading trips to the South Pacific to find confirmation of what happened. Founded by a former investigator of modern aircraft crashes, the organization boasts a solid pedigree, but it also has many critics. Its researchers claim to be open to others disproving their findings. TIGHAR spent twenty-five years studying one piece of evidence; a piece of metal they hoped was part of Earhart's plane. In a space as vast as the Pacific Ocean, for a piece of metal that appears enough like that of Earhart's plane to be from a different plane seems very strange. As TIGHAR wrote, is it too much of a coincidence that "this incredibly specific, but random, piece of debris just happened to end up on Nikumaroro, the atoll where so much other evidence points to Earhart"?

TIGHAR search crews have found a pocket knife, bottles, zippers, and pieces of a shoe. They have a jar that may have contained Dr. Berry's Freckle Ointment, and since Earhart was known to not like her freckles, perhaps the lightener could be hers. All of this "could mean just about anything" because people have lived on the island at different times. Military forces have also visited, and Nikumaroro sits near two currents, right in the path to receive and hold on its shores all sorts of garbage that had been bobbing around the ocean, originating from around the world. TIGHAR has found bones that could be human or turtle. The DNA results are still inconclusive. Even now, scientists are unable to unlock this tricky mystery.

Some researchers believe these pieces of aircraft and shoes are evidence of Amelia Earhart's crash site.

The Oldest Transportation Dream

The dream of flight may not be as old as fire, but it could be older than the invention of the wheel. This is fascinating since we all know carts and carriages were around way before the first successful modern airplane. Yet there are indications that humans may have been dreaming of flying in a machine long before they had the technology and know-how to build one.

In 2015, archaeologists found cave paintings in China dating as far back as ten thousand years ago depicting shapes similar to modern aircraft. In 2014, archaeologists found cave art from a similar time period that some suggest may depict UFOs. Could knowledge of flight be that old? Unfortunately, we may never know the answer. Scientists agree these drawings could represent something entirely different from aircraft.

While we cannot be certain of what exactly the cave dwellers were painting, we do know that people throughout history dreamed and attempted flight. Back in ninth-century Córdoba, Spain, it is reported that Abbas Qasim ibn Firnas successfully glided wearing "wings." In the fifteenth century, Leonardo da Vinci sketched an **ornithopter**, a machine imitating a bird, with flapping "wings."

Such a design is better suited to birds. Humans are simply much too large to achieve sustained flight with wings. The next design to come along, in the late eighteenth century, was similar to a hot-air balloon without any controls for direction. It

This millennia-old rock image in northwest China looks like an aircraft.

wasn't until the turn of the nineteenth century that the concept of the airplane was born. Sir George Cayley came up with the idea of fixed wings, a propulsion system, and movable control surfaces. Cayley also calculated the forces of lift and drag. He showed his work as a kite on a stick with a movable tail. A young boy was the first to put Cayley's design into practice, in 1849.

By 1866, there was an aircraft society, the Royal Aeronautical Society in England, and two years later an exhibition of aircraft.

France's Alphonse Pénaud invented and used "the torsion motor," which harnessed the power of twisted rubber bands, to fly a 20-inch-long (51-centimeter) plane 131 feet (40 meters) in eleven seconds. This was the first flight of a stable, powered aircraft. In 1874, the Du Temple brothers, also of France, got the first manned and powered fixed-wing airplane to not quite fly but at least ... hop.

Others around the world continued to work toward the skies, until finally Orville Wright made the first powered, sustained, and manned flight in a fully controllable aircraft, on December 17, 1903. Orville won a coin toss with his brother and close business partner, Wilbur, which is how he ended up in the history books as the first person to fly. Earhart was only six years old at that time, but she and the brothers would become friends. The Library of Congress has letters exchanged between Earhart and Orville from 1932 and 1934. More than three decades after those letters, in 1969, another flight pioneer, Neil Armstrong, took the first steps on the moon, with a piece of fabric from the wing of the Wright brothers' 1903 plane and a piece of wood from the plane's propeller in his pocket.

Other bones of interest have also been found. In the 1990s, a World War II historian found a file on the "Discovery of Human Remains on Gardner Island." Considering the measurements recorded of the bones, they could be male. They could also be female, in which case their proportions might match Earhart's, based on her photos. Only 20 percent of American women have those proportions, narrowing the pool of whom they could have belonged to, which in turn has led people to imagine they could be Earhart's. Unfortunately, the bones themselves have gone missing, if they existed at all.

This is, at the least, positive for Earhart's image in the world's collective memory. If the latest clues are correct, Earhart may not have crashed at sea. Instead, she may have landed her plane, perhaps without loss of life, and even kept the craft intact enough to continue sending SOS signals from one steady location for five days after disappearing. The signs of life on land could mean Earhart kept her cool and likely made good decisions like a skilled pilot should.

four

A Controversial Legacy

***"When they fail, their failure must be but a challenge to others."* —Amelia Earhart**

Earhart was celebrated, idolized, and mythologized long before her death. Even her routine practice flights drew crowds, and major flights were met with parades. She could not have made the lasting impression she did without the admiration of many for her work, her opinions, her connections, and her persona.

Perhaps another reason for her lasting fame is that her success has been widely debated. In fact, some of Earhart's longest-lasting critics have been other female pilots. Many who knew her, or flew at the same time she did, considered

Opposite: Amelia Earhart is greeted with a ticker-tape parade upon her return from a flight.

her a dilettante, interested in flying more as a hobby than as a serious profession. Pilots of today lament her celebrity because her legend overshadows other pilots who achieved just as much, if not more, as Earhart.

Critics and Competition

Richard Gillespie, who wrote *Finding Amelia*, said, in his professional opinion as a former airline crash investigator, Earhart was an "average" pilot. Neta Snook, now known simply as Earhart's instructor, was an accomplished aviatrix herself and the first woman aviator to run her own airfield. Although her opinion changed over time, at first Snook didn't believe Earhart was a "natural" and, therefore, would not be a great pilot. Even during Earhart's life, people saw her as "something of a show-boater, a fame-lover, whose PR and connections helped her eclipse the achievements of less glamorous and more dedicated female pilots."

Captain Hilton Railey may have helped secure Earhart's first big gig, but he disagreed with her plan for her last flight. He wrote on the one-year anniversary of Earhart's disappearance that "she was caught up in the hero racket which compelled her to strive for increasingly dramatic records, bigger and braver feats that automatically insured the publicity necessary to the maintenance of her position as the foremost woman pilot in the world."

The Flying Flapper of Freeport

Earhart seemed to receive lopsided attention compared to Elinor Smith, who flew at the same time as Earhart and was considered a rival. Smith, from Freeport, Long Island, was

Elinor Smith was considered a top pilot, but people were often just as interested in her fashion and personality.

also one of the 117 licensed female pilots the Ninety-Nines organization was created for. She, too, faced sexism in the industry. While neither Earhart nor Smith was forced to work celebrity angles, in a way they did have to in order stay employed and be employable as women in aviation. So, Smith welcomed her image on a Wheaties box in 1934, and she accepted nicknames in the tabloids such as Long Island's "youthful air queen," "intrepid birdwoman," and "the flying flapper." She also risked trouble with federal-level authorities when, on a male chauvinist's dare, she flew under all four New York City East River bridges.

Smith and Earhart differed in their skills as pilots. At age sixteen, Smith became the youngest licensed pilot in the world. Fellow aviators voted Smith female pilot of the year, over Earhart, in 1930. Yet Earhart achieved much greater fame during her career, perhaps due to Putnam. Upon Smith's death, the *Washington Post* quoted her son Patrick H. Sullivan III as saying Earhart was not the first pilot Putnam admired. Sullivan claimed George Putman was trying to make money off any female flier, but none would accept the contracts heavily weighted in his favor, until Earhart. It was Putnam who pulled all the strings he could for Earhart. According to Sullivan, on the one occasion Smith did accept Putnam's money to make a record-breaking flight, but upon her landing, Putnam switched her out for Earhart, and the latter would receive the accolades. "Amelia's fame was largely puffery, and the other female pilots resented the hell out of it," Sullivan said.

Costly Search Efforts

Critics even blamed Earhart for the expense of the crews and equipment that were sent out to find and rescue her on the authorization of President Franklin Delano Roosevelt. People were resentful that Earhart had knowingly set out on what seemed to them a dangerous joyride. It was her fault for doing something so foolish that could require rescuers. Reports put the rescue cost at $250,000 a day, totaling $4 million. Additionally, dangerous tropical weather systems sometimes forced rescue planes to land. At one time, sixty US Navy planes were looking for Earhart's plane, with 1,500 sailors on the mission because they were based on the aircraft carrier from which the rescue planes flew.

After this, the most expensive air and sea search in history at that time, Congress considered making it illegal for the navy to search for lost flights that had taken off with no scientific or commercial purpose. "From now on no individual will be permitted to take off on any ocean or round-the-world flight that smacks of a stunt," Assistant Secretary of Commerce John Monroe Johnson told *Time* magazine.

Even Earhart seemed to offer herself a bit of weary criticism in one of her last conversations before her fateful flight. Carl

Allen, the aviation correspondent for the *Herald Tribune*, who'd covered Earhart's entire career and who'd come to be her friend, told her he put her odds at succeeding at fifty-fifty. In an uncharacteristically vain and morbid comment, she replied, "As far as I know I've only got one obsession—a small and probably typically feminine horror of growing old—so I won't feel completely cheated if I fail to come back." Her next birthday, on July 24th, which she should have celebrated upon her return, would have been her fortieth. Instead, the search for her body was officially closed six days before. Maybe, as Railey would write on the anniversary of her death, "she was a victim of the era of 'hot' aeronautics which began with Colonel Lindbergh and Admiral Byrd and which shot 'scientific' expeditions across continents, oceans and polar regions by dint of individual exhibition."

Breaking the Glass Ceiling

Pilots, regardless of gender, face issues unique to their career that are both physically and mentally challenging. As a female pilot, Earhart faced many different layers of obstacles, and she was not alone in that. Women were not often welcome in the "boys' club" that was (and still is) aviation; if they did break in, they were treated differently, and not for the better.

New Zealand native Jean Batten, who received her pilot's license in 1932, seemed to have it all: flying skill, ability, and determination; a sparkling personality; good looks; the attention of celebrities and royalty; and the romantic attention of wealthy, powerful male admirers. Yet she wrote often in her flight journals of severe loneliness. Imagine spending days, if not weeks, flying alone. All pilots must face that. Now imagine doing that as

Fashion to Fund Flying

As a child exploring and climbing trees, no one would have expected fashion stardom from little "Millie" Earhart, but she did, at least for a time, influence how society viewed style and dress for women. The media helped shape public perception of Earhart's look as feminine and functional. "Hers is the healthy curiosity of the clean mind and the strong body … She will become a symbol of new womanhood," one writer said at the time of Earhart's style.

Earhart needed financial support for her flying, and people seemed curious about her style. She did own a sewing machine, and she had experience making her own clothes. She may have even had some genuine personal interest in fashion. Early in her career, she was teased by other pilots over how shiny and new her leather flying coat was, so she aged it by sleeping in it and staining it with a little aircraft oil. She made some samples, and the designs for her fashion line were shaped by her concept of functionality and simplicity. The clothes labeled with her signature were found in about thirty cities and were sold in select department stores such as R. H. Macy & Co. and Strawbridge & Clothier.

Amelia Earhart Fashions was one of the first clothing lines to be created by a celebrity. Unfortunately, the business wasn't as successful as Earhart's flying. Its affordable beauty, inspired by aviation, with practical separates and washable fabrics, did not take off as Earhart hoped. Perhaps the economic impact of the Great Depression prevented women from purchasing

Amelia Earhart models a flannel Norfolk jacket and checked tweed skirt that she designed.

the clothes and reaching "new altitudes," as the line's tagline suggested it would.

Yet Earhart's fashion did have long-reaching influence. In the spring of 2011, designer Jean Paul Gaultier's ready-to-wear fashion line appeared to be inspired by Earhart's own day-to-day look, though the designer didn't fully realize it. "I was inspired by a woman, I forgot her name, an American pilot with very short, wavy hair who was wearing an aviator jacket, which I love, and a little scarf that was *so* Hermes," Gaultier said. Earhart's fashion line, which lasted barely three years, was supposed to add to her fame; decades later, her style is still remembered and revived, even by people who do not know her name.

A year after her induction into the Arizona Aviation Hall of Fame, ninety-two-year-old Ruby Sheldon was still flying.

a woman, knowing that even once you step down from the cockpit, you will not always be among supporters. You will be faced with criticisms based solely on your sex.

Female aviators who fought to fly had to cling to their work and continue to battle, even after breaking into the industry. Ruby Wine Sheldon, born in 1917, held the first helicopter instrument instructor certificate ever issued by the FAA. Over her decades-long career, she logged more than 15,000 flight hours in a variety of craft, was inducted into the Arizona Aviation Hall of Fame, and was honored with an exhibit in the Smithsonian Air and Space Museum. Yet after World War II, almost no companies would hire female pilots, she said. She took the job offered by the one company that would, flying cargo helicopters off of ice floes in the Arctic Circle. She'd come to love her work with the US Geological Survey, piloting remote sensing missions from the Panama Canal to Alaska. She was still flying in her eighties and nineties. When something is so hard to come by, you can't easily let it go.

Woman or Pilot

It might be most accurate to call Earhart an enigma. She was prolific in her flying but also in her acts of celebrity. She was outspoken and independent, but also seemingly under some guidance from her husband. She didn't have what people of the day considered a "womanly" figure; nevertheless, she ran a fashion line. She was a woman, yet she was a pilot. She was not easily categorized.

Judith Thurman wrote in the *New Yorker*, "Putnam, the press, and, no doubt, Earhart herself were aware that there was something troubling about her appearance that had to be neutralized." Photo spreads of her in magazines, no rarity for a media sensation such as Earhart, often jarringly juxtaposed shots of her in pants and course heavy materials with ones of her wearing long skirts, even evening gowns, her arms overflowing with flowers. This was merely one way that Earhart didn't fit neatly into a social category, but it also points to the larger perplexity that swirled around her. In many ways, it's no different than what we see today. In general, society likes people to fit into simple definitions, and unique individuals are often met with criticism, anger, and judgment. In the case of Earhart, the media and the public attempted to define and understand her seemingly dual nature: woman or pilot. Yet the truth is that there is no one single categorical truth for any person, let alone a trailblazer like Earhart.

Greta Garbo of the Skies

Jean Batten was considered the greatest long-distance pilot at the time Earhart was flying. She did not just set records for female pilots, but for all pilots. In 1935, Earhart and Batten shared the honor of the International Harmon Trophy for their stellar individual work. While the competition bothered Earhart's husband, George Putnam, it excited Earhart to compete against someone so skilled, and it fueled her to keep buying new equipment and work to perform at a consistently higher level. Kathleen C. Winters, aviation historian and herself a licensed pilot, states in her book *Amelia Earhart: The Turbulent Life of an American Icon* that Earhart herself said that Batten's "flights were an inspiration to all women."

Born in New Zealand in 1909, Batten started toward a career as a concert pianist, but after a discussion with pilot Charles Kingsford Smith, who knew her father, Batten was hooked on the idea of flying. She convinced people to lend her money or even to give her planes. She was called "the Greta Garbo of the skies," meaning she had the allure of the famous Hollywood actress, so she could convince people to do things for her. Four years after earning her license in 1932, she had broken records, secured a book deal, and been named a Commander of the Order of the British Empire for her trailblazing work in her field.

Batten's first major records were indeed impressive. Her first record-breaking attempt was to challenge that of Amy Johnson, who had flown by herself in 1930 from England to Australia

Jean Batten, pictured in 1934, competed against men and women to set many long-distance flying records.

in twenty days. On her third attempt, starting on May 8, 1934, Batten succeeded, making the trip in fourteen days, twenty-two hours. Batten then had to get back to England. Topping off her recent accomplishment with another, by making the round trip, she became the first woman to fly that route.

Her next feat would break a record held by Jim Mollison, who interestingly was married to Amy Johnson at the time. Mollison had flown in early 1933 from England to Senegal to Brazil in eighty-five hours, twenty minutes, becoming the first person to fly solo across both the North and the South

Atlantic. Late in 1935, Batten made the trip (specifically, France to Morocco to Brazil) in sixty-one hours, fifteen minutes, a whole day faster than Mollison.

Among her many honors, Batten was awarded honorary military recognition in the air force in three countries: Great Britain, France, and Brazil. She was also the first woman to receive the industry's highest honor in 1938: the medal of the Fédération Aéronautique Internationale.

Women in the Races

Sometimes it's difficult to tell, through the lens of history, if two people were friends or rivals, if one inspired the other, or if they just worked in parallel and weren't particularly moved by each other. We do know that not only was Louise Thaden a good friend of Earhart's, but their relationship may have been a little of all of the above: friendship and friendly rivalry, full of mutual respect and inspiration.

Thaden worked her way into the boys' club of aviation from the inside, as an office manager for Beech Aircraft. She took flying lessons there, soloing in 1928. Later that year, she

This 1930 photo of Louise Thaden was taken the year after she won the first all-women transcontinental air race.

became the first American woman to hold the world's altitude record for women, flying above 20,000 feet (6,096 m). In 1929, she set the solo flight endurance record and the woman's world speed record. Earhart also held at different times these altitude and speed records and, as an elected official of the National Aeronautic Association, had lobbied the Fédération Aéronautique Internationale (which monitored record setting) to establish three separate record categories for women: altitude, speed, and endurance. Earhart and Thaden both held the records at different times. Though Thaden, the only woman to ever hold all three of those records simultaneously, bested Earhart, she wouldn't have been able to if Earhart had not pushed for the records to exist. Their relationship to each other—collaborative and competitive—was tangled.

Later in 1929, Thaden won the first Women's Air Derby, and in the process she beat Earhart, who took third place. Gladys O'Donnell took second. Earhart had helped to organize the race in order to demonstrate that women could fly in difficult, stressful conditions. Again, without Earhart, there may not have been a race for Thaden to beat her in. The goal was to demonstrate that women were indeed just as capable pilots as men, and in 1935, Earhart was one of two women to enter the Bendix Trophy Race.

The transcontinental air contest between Cleveland, Ohio, and Los Angeles, California, had previously been seen as no place for female competitors. Earhart's arrival at the finish line was a disappointment, since she placed fifth. However, her flight back to Cleveland beat by two hours the nonstop flight record she had set the previous year. In 1936, Thaden entered the Bendix.

As Thaden crossed the finish line, she thought the crowd was going wild because she'd arrived from the wrong direction. Despite the technological advancements and record-setting flights, aviators were still risking expensive equipment and their very lives in what was still the early days of flying. Thaden and her copilot, Blanche Noyes, were also at a disadvantage because the radio had gone out, and the setting sun and smoke from nearby forest fires had made it impossible to see. They were forced to make the approach in reverse, because it was in this way they could determine where they were. Imagine how surprised they were to learn the reason for the cheering: they had won, against men and women aviators alike. For this impressive success, Thaden later received the Harmon Trophy, which Earhart had already won three times in a row.

five

Earhart's Lasting Impact

"Women must try to do things as men have tried. When they fail, their failure must be but a challenge to others." —Amelia Earhart

It is impossible for us to look into the past and find out exactly what the real Earhart was like. We can read accounts by those who knew her and make assumptions about her as a person, an aviator, and a celebrity, but all of those perspectives are written through the lens of bias. Just as we infer things after watching one interview with a celebrity today, or decide we know someone after meeting them once, opinions can be formed based on very little real information. While it is interesting to read the multiple perspectives on Earhart, it is incredibly

Opposite: Patrouille de France, an aerobatics team, releases colored smoke over Paris on Bastille Day in 2016.

important that we remember those accounts are not the whole truth, and may not even add up to truth.

The sexism that Earhart and other women of her generation faced still haunts American society. Women are encouraged to take certain classes in school, which means they're less likely to be qualified for jobs in male-dominated fields. When a woman does choose a career in an industry characterized as male, she will often endure harassment and close scrutiny. Furthermore, women still face a gender pay gap. In media, women face conflicting images of what they should and should not be. Even the very toys and clothes marketed for boys and girls send the message that they are different and should have distinctive roles. Women are expected to fulfill duties at home, yet they are looked down upon if they don't have a job. They are expected to lead at work, but they are scorned or met with disbelief if they do not have children. It is almost impossible for a woman to attempt a so-called work/life balance, accused of being too soft or too hard, and criticized for cheating one area of life for the other.

It is worth examining the aviatrixes of the past, for we must acknowledge and appreciate that they led the way for modern-day aviation leaders. Without the impact of Earhart and her contemporaries, the following women may not have accomplished their amazing feats, regardless of their gender.

Suzanne Asbury: Writing Her Legacy in the Clouds

Born more than half a century after Earhart, Suzanne Asbury (now Suzanne Asbury-Oliver) still managed to secure her spot as an aviation pioneer. She became the first female skywriter.

In fact, at the time of this book, she is still the one and only! Skywriting, once a popular form of advertising, is rare today, though Asbury-Oliver, along with her husband, continue working in the field.

Asbury-Oliver started flying at age fourteen, soloing at age fifteen, in Oregon. In the early 1980s, when she was starting to look for her first job as an adult, she saw an ad that Pepsi was looking for a skywriter. Although she had never done such a thing before, she figured she knew enough about flying to figure it out. Additionally, the major commercial airlines were in a slump at the time, and she doubted she'd be able to find work with them. Sometimes, out of scarcity comes opportunity.

She apprenticed with Jack Strayer, the Pepsi skywriter at the time, and when he retired a year later, she became the company's go-to pilot. Pepsi advertised its product with skywriting from 1932 to 2000. Now that her primary employer is no longer using skywriting, Asbury-Oliver offers her services for single events: marriage proposals, concert tour announcements, and congratulations messages. She writes more than 500 messages in over 150 locations yearly.

There is a tradition of secrecy in skywriting that dates back to the time when there was a lot of competition in the field. The technique reached it's popularity in the 1930s and 1940s. Pilots couldn't risk sharing what type of fluid or exhaust pump they used. Asbury-Oliver follows that tradition of staying mum about the equipment details, though she will share some stories about the job. She writes the letters 10,000 feet (3,048 m) above the ground. Her 1956 de Havilland Chipmunk plane, which she and her husband modified with a 27-gallon (102-liter) smoke oil system, ups the number of letters she can write in a flight from the standard of ten to twenty-five.

Once, Asbury-Oliver and her husband had a near run-in with an F-16 fighter aircraft. They'd been hired by an antiwar activist to write "PEACE NOW" above the 2008 Democratic National Convention. During their first pass on writing "PEACE," the security team told them they were close to the airspace guarded by F-16s. The skywriters had been cleared to write their message near that restricted air zone, but if they actually entered it, the F-16s would come after them. So they adjusted their plans and made the turn within 0.3 miles (0.5 km) of the zone.

There is a lot of preparation and expense involved in message writing. For one, skywriting fluid is very expensive. Asbury-Oliver and her plane also need to travel to the message location. Even to ask someone to prom could cost multiple thousands of dollars. Asbury-Oliver has written messages in multiple alphabets and using non-letter shapes, which at times can take some time planning in order to get unfamiliar symbols looking just right. Moreover, she has to schedule around the weather. Wind, of course, can throw a skywriting plan off. A message could become alphabet soup on a windy day. Plus, Asbury-Oliver takes a lot of pride in her work and likes to make sure the sun hits the letters just right, illuminating the message but not blinding the audience. With the right conditions, the message can last for whole afternoons, sometimes drifting hundreds of miles, being viewed by people in multiple cities.

Patricia Cowings: Sky-High Smarts

Patricia Cowings definitely makes the list of those who followed Earhart's wake into the skies of the modern era. Cowings was the first American woman to be trained by NASA as a scientist astronaut. Earhart would probably have liked Cowings' determination. While in graduate school, Cowlings wrote a letter to a hero of hers, Neal Miller, a pioneer in biofeedback research, asking if she could work for him. From that simple, direct request, a career was born. Though she's never blasted off in a spaceship, Cowings was an alternate for a 1979 mission into space, and she has earned honors and awards due to her aerospace contributions.

With her psychology degree, Cowings researched "space sickness," the psycho-physiological and biological problems astronauts can experience in space. She designed and patented a program that trains astronauts to control automatic functions like heart rate and breathing rate. If an astronaut masters this autogenic-feedback training exercise (AFTE), he or she can control up to twenty seemingly uncontrollable body reactions in order to overcome motion sickness, even under high stress, and still be able to perform duties at a high level.

Jeana Yeager: Around the World Without a Breath

Earhart died trying to set the record at the time for flying the longest route around the world. Nearly fifty years after Earhart disappeared, American pilot Jeana Yeager broke one of the last circumnavigation barriers and flew around the world nonstop and without refueling.

On December 14, 1986, copilots Yeager and Dick Rutan took off from Edwards Air Force Base in Southern California in a plane of their own design called the *Voyager*. Nine days, three minutes, forty-two seconds later, they arrived back at Edwards. They were challenged the entire flight. Not only did they face

Jeana Yeager poses with her copilot, Dick Rutan, after a test flight for their successful flight around the world.

mechanical and weather scares, but they survived it all in a cockpit the size of a phone booth. For their accomplishment, they received aviation's highest award, the Collier Trophy.

Yeager and Rutan first came up with the original design over lunch with Burt Rutan, Dick's brother, in 1981, and they actually sketched their idea on napkins. Both Yeager and Dick helped with the concept and building the plane, but Burt served as the main project engineer. His biggest challenge was to find materials that were both super light and super strong. The plane had to move efficiently over a long and challenging distance, and if the flight was to be nonstop, it also had to be able to hold all that fuel.

In the end, made of graphite, Kevlar, and fiberglass, the *Voyager* weighed only about 939 pounds (426 kilograms) until they added fuel, and then it jumped up to an incredible 9,700 pounds (4,400 kg). The plane was tested over eighteen months, with the pilots and volunteers clocking a total of twenty-two thousand hours. On December 14, 1987, their creation, that plane, was hung in the Smithsonian.

Patty Wagstaff: Aerobatic Savant

Earhart decided that flying was her life's mission after watching one air-stunt show, and sixty-three years later, in 1983, Patty Wagstaff had a similar revelation. She witnessed her first **aerobatics** show and immediately said to herself, "I can do that!" Five years after she'd earned her pilot's license, Wagstaff was on the US Aerobatic Team. She became the first woman to take the US National Aerobatic Championship, in 1991, and she defended her title for the next two years.

Aerobatic figures, or maneuvers, are loops, spins, dives, abrupt changes in direction, and the like. Some of them have great names: the Avalanche, the Hammerhead, the Humpty-Bump, the Reverse Half Cuban Eight, and the English Bunt, to name a few. It sounds like a relatively recent sport, but even the Wright brothers technically performed an aerobatic move. In 1904, they completed a 360-degree banked turn. Today, the necessary work to complete this movement would be handled by little panels on the tops of the fixed wings of modern planes. Back then, the brothers Wright had to manually tilt the entire wings. To perform extreme gravity-defying and death-defying entertaining moves was not the Wrights' goal, of course (simple flying was wild enough back then), so we should consider the barnstormers of the 1910s and 1920s as the actual aerobatics innovators.

Earhart's first teacher, Neta Snook, began her career in flying as a barnstormer. What started as simple exhibitions of flight grew mundane for pilots and audiences, and the demand for more exciting feats of flight increased. For example, Lincoln Beachey became famous for his "death dip." At 5,000 feet (1,524 m) above the ground, he cut his plane's engine and free-fell, nose pointed straight at the ground rushing up to meet him, pulling up only at the very last possible moment.

It was Wagstaff's dad who introduced her to planes. He was a captain for Japan Airlines and let his daughter take the controls of his DC-6 when she was only ten years old. Her first job as a licensed pilot was with the Bristol Bay Native Association in Alaska. She traveled to villages so remote they are accessible only by airplanes. She continues to work in remote areas, at different times training pilots in the Kenya Wildlife Service and serving with Cal Fire as an air attack pilot, supporting California wildfire fighters.

Wagstaff was inducted into the National Aviation Hall of Fame in 2004, but she is perhaps proudest of having received the airshow industry's most prestigious awards, the Sword of Excellence and the Bill Barber Award for Showmanship. Now, she runs her own aerobatics school, the Patty Wagstaff Aerobatic School, in Florida. Not that long ago, women were banned from schools that taught flying, and now they're running them.

Her aerobatics plane, the Goodrich Extra 260, has found its final home on display in the Smithsonian National Air and Space Museum.

Sally Ride: First Woman in Space

Of all the women who followed Amelia Earhart into the sky, perhaps the woman with the most exciting claim is Sally Ride. On June 18, 1983, she became the first American woman in space, as well as the youngest American ever in space, at age thirty-two. Ride flew two missions for NASA on space shuttle *Challenger*, and she served on the investigation committee following both the 1986 *Challenger* tragedy and the 2003 *Columbia* crash.

She almost didn't make that history, though. She dropped out of Swarthmore College, where she was a physics major, in 1969, to be a full-time tennis player. Before college, she had been ranked eighteenth in the nation. Thankfully, she soon returned to school, this time to Stanford University, where she double-majored in English literature and physics. Not only did Ride love math and science, both considered subjects better suited for men, but she also did decidedly "unladylike" things in her spare time, as Earhart had. In addition to being a tennis champion, Ride was also an obsessive street football player.

Ride was perplexed by the box society wanted to force her as a woman into. She was a scientist who'd passed every rigorous mental and physical test her male colleagues had passed to be chosen for a mission into space. Yet the questions she received from reporters were about the safety of her reproductive organs, whether or not she would wear a bra in space, and her likelihood of crying on the mission. Late-night comedians joked that she'd hold up the liftoff because she'd be fretting about her outfit. One male Soviet **cosmonaut** welcomed her on the space station by directing her toward the kitchen.

Earhart and Ride share so many other similarities that perhaps if she'd survived her last flight, Earhart would have gone on to influence others, like Ride did after her retirement from flying. Before her death in 2012 of pancreatic cancer, Ride continued to inspire others as a professor of physics, and she led outreach programs. She also wrote six science books for kids and developed school programs and materials "to make science and engineering cool again," especially for girls.

Amelia Earhart: Finally Traveling the Globe!

"In the best way we knew how, we brought Amelia's spirit home safely to Oakland." That was a tweet sent by Amelia Earhart on July 12, 2014.

It was on that day Amelia Rose Earhart, no relation to Amelia Mary Earhart, became the youngest woman to circumnavigate the globe in a single-engine aircraft, a Pilatus PC-12. Between June 26 and July 12, the thirty-one-year-old and her copilot covered more than 24,000 miles (38,624 km) and made seventeen stops. This Earhart had no navigation issues. Though equipped with modern advances such as dual GPS, she did skip autopilot and flew the plane herself the whole way, just like her namesake would have.

That flight paid homage to Earhart in name. Nearly twenty years before, another woman paid homage to her as well. In 1997, overlapping with what would have been Earhart's one-hundredth birthday, Linda Finch completed Earhart's exact planned route around the globe.

Peggy Whitson: Age Knows No Altitude

Launching from Kazakhstan (a country bordered by the Caspian Sea, China, and Russia) on November 18, 2016, at 2:20 a.m. local time (midday November 17 in New York City), Peggy Whitson broke more than one aviation record: she became the first woman to command the **International Space Station** two separate times, and she became the oldest woman to travel to space. At that time she was fifty-six years old; she celebrated her next birthday, on February 9, 2017, while still in space.

Whitson's story of becoming a pilot, and then later an astronaut, is yet another one of determination and persistence, of pushing through both financial obstacles and discrimination. Born in 1960 on a farm in rural Iowa, Whitson may have seemed an unlikely candidate for life in the skies. At that time, it was still rare to be a passenger on a commercial flight. Women were rarely on planes, unless serving as flight attendants, and they certainly were not in the cockpit. Whitson's life would have been a lot different had her father not obtained his private pilot's license when she was ten and taken her on her first plane ride. From that moment on, she knew her career path was in aviation.

While her parents kept growing soybeans and raising hogs, Whitson started her own flock of chickens, which she sold at two dollars a piece. With this "chicken money," she paid for school and flight time to earn her own private pilot's license. As a young adult, Whitson connected with James

The Greatest Race *Above* Earth

Interest in and experimentation with aviation started well before Amelia Earhart was born; even a few other women, not just men, beat her to the cockpit. Yet women's air racing kicked off alongside Earhart's career, in 1929, with the Women's Air Derby. That year, twenty pilots flew from Santa Monica, California, to Cleveland, Ohio. Earhart was one of them, though she did not win.

The race is still held annually. It was put on hold once, during World War II, and has changed names over the years, from the Women's Air Derby; to the All Women's Transcontinental Air Race, or the Powder Puff Derby; to the Air Race Classic (ARC), as it's been known since 1977. Throughout it all, the event

Louise Thaden (*far left*) won the first Women's Air Derby, 1929, and Amelia Earhart (*fourth from the right*) placed third.

Abbie Pasmore (*left*) and Emmy Dillon won the 2016 Air Race Classic.

has served to educate people about the future of women in aviation while preserving their tradition.

On June 21, 2016, 130 pilots left Prescott, Arizona, for Daytona Beach, Florida. They had four days to travel 2,700 miles (4,345 km). By the rules, they could have been as young as seventeen at takeoff or as old as ninety. They flew in teams of at least two, and while of course all were licensed pilots, many also had other careers: there was a Pulitzer Prize winner, three teams of families, a nurse, school teachers, retirees, and nineteen teams of college students. Emmy Dillon and Abbie Pasmore, both from Embry-Riddle Aeronautical University, were team Riddle Racer Gold, and they took the gold medal. Second place went to the Flying Sycamores: Lydia Kost, Kayleigh Bordner, and MiJin Kim, from Indiana State University. Bordner, who had competed before, told the ARC: "I participate in the Air Race Classic to pay tribute to the women who paved the way for younger pilots like myself."

Peggy Whitson (*right*) greets Pam Melroy after the shuttle *Discovery* docked at the International Space Station in 2007.

Van Allen, a physicist and fellow Iowan who was himself a pioneer in space exploration. She told him of her plan to be an astronaut, but he did not think that it would be a good long-term profession. Whitson was not deterred, even though Van Allen was considered knowledgeable in the field. Today she is an expert in an industry that continues to make important advancements.

Astronauts that NASA sends to the International Space Station use the lab to improve our understanding about living in space. Whitson believes this to be the ultimate objective: "In terms of goals for NASA before I die, we need to be living on Mars. And I might not live that long, so they better get with it!" When she launched as part of Expedition 50/51 in November of 2016, Whitson already held the record for longest time spent in space by a woman, 377 days. In total, she had spent more than a year in space. By the end of her most recent mission, which was six months long with a return to Earth in spring of 2017, Whitson surpassed all American astronauts' time in space. Man or woman, no American has lived in space longer than Whitson.

The Ninety-Nines: Still Flying Proud

From its small but mighty beginnings in 1929, the Ninety-Nines is now an organization that is way more than ninety-nine members strong. It has more than 150 chapters in the United States and Canada alone. Its education programs and curricula help future female pilots, and its museum preserves and promotes the successes of those from the past.

Wanted: More Pilots

If you are interested and succeed in your schooling to become a pilot, there's room for you in the skies. The United States, and the world in general, is poised on the brink of another turning point in aviation, as a severe pilot shortage is likely, but relatively new education requirements make training incredibly expensive.

An airline consultant has estimated that nearly one-fifth of pilots for major US airlines will retire by 2020, three-fifths by 2030. Boeing, a leading manufacturer of commercial jets, has said that the world will soon need more than half a million new pilots. Unfortunately, retirement is not the only reason that eleven of twelve regional airlines report having a difficult time finding pilots, according to a 2014 US Government Accountability Office study. The system no longer works, and people trying to build careers as pilots are not always successful.

In the past, a person might learn how to fly in the military. Upon returning to civilian life, he or she would copilot and then pilot for a regional airline, eventually moving on to a major airline. This all worked smoothly because flying was becoming commonplace. The average person could afford a ticket, which increased the number of flights and pilots needed, which made flying even more accessible, which increased the numbers yet again. However, flight schools and acquiring flight time is costly, and pilots must spend a certain amount of hours in the air before they can work for an airline. In order to expand the number of eligible candidates, airlines lowered required flight times for new hirees 350 hours for pilots and 250 hours for copilots.

After the crash of Colgan Air Flight 3407 in 2009, which killed forty-nine people, and the subsequent Congressional mandate in the Airline Safety and Federal Aviation Administration Extension Act of 2010, a pilot now needs a minimum 1,000 flight hours as a copilot in air carrier operations before he or she can serve as a captain.

The military is turning away from manned aircrafts and toward drones, so it's harder to get a start in the business from that direction. A graduate of aviation college has a pilot's license and about 300 hours of flight time. That person must go on to log 1,200 more hours, often costing more than $100 an hour.

There's Still Room to Improve

Unfortunately, diversity in the aviation industry as a whole hasn't progressed much since Earhart's time. Women make up about 6 percent of American pilots. The lack of support for females in the industry is clear from grade school through career. Girls are not encouraged from a young age to learn mechanical systems like boys are. It could be argued girls are even discouraged from such activities. This can leave them unqualified for many flight schools. If they do secure jobs, they regularly face harassment or discrimination. Yet when they do break into the field, they often more than prove their worth. For example, women make up 10 percent of US Army

In 2015, Rebekah M. Wottge was an Apache helicopter pilot with the Thirty-Fourth Combat Aviation Brigade.

Apache helicopter pilots, but they account for only 3 percent of accidents, zero if they are working in all-female crews.

At her core, Earhart wanted to be a pilot, and she accomplished that goal. Despite the rudimentary aviation technology and mechanics of the day, and despite, most of all, the sexism she faced, she overcame the odds and even lived the way she wanted to. Earhart was criticized for doing things to stay in the spotlight, but she wouldn't have gotten funding for flying or aviation opportunities if she didn't make herself a marketable commodity. It is possible she wasn't a prodigy, but that does not mean she wasn't a good pilot. Even though some doubted her flying skills, she consistently set records throughout her career. Whether it was her celebrity status or her mysterious disappearance, whether for her fashion or her flying, Earhart certainly was a fearless woman whose legacy lives on.

Glossary

aerobatics Acrobatics performed in the air.

aeronautics The science or practice of air travel.

aviation The operation of an aircraft.

aviator A pilot of an aircraft.

aviatrix A woman who is a pilot; an old-fashioned term no longer used.

barnstorming A form of entertainment offered by airplane pilots. Individuals, or groups called flying circuses, would offer to fly passengers on short trips and perform stunt flying exhibitions. Popular in the rural Midwest in the 1920s.

corset An undergarment tightly fitting the chest, stomach, and hips, worn to shape the body into a desired figure.

cosmonaut The Russian name for "astronaut."

International Space Station Spacecraft that orbits Earth, 220 miles (254 km) above the planet. It's both a science lab and a home for astronauts spending a long time in space. Many countries collaborated to build it, so now they all are allowed to use it.

Jim Crow laws State and local laws that enforced racial segregation and discrimination.

jodhpur Pants for wearing while riding horses.

ornithopter A machine imitating a bird, with flapping "wings"; the first "aircraft" envisioned by humans.

Progressive Era A time of response to the economic and social problems of rapid industrialization in America, lasting from the late 1800s through the 1920s.

science fiction Fiction based on an imagined future of scientific advances and social changes.

spinster An unmarried woman, usually one older than "marrying age"; an old-fashioned term no longer used.

stunt flying Dangerous moves performed for entertainment in an aircraft.

telegraph A system that uses making and breaking an electrical connection to transmit messages.

ticker-tape parade A parade celebrating a hero or visiting dignitary during which people in office buildings lining the route throw confetti (originally, the streamer-like paper that stock quotes were printed on).

transatlantic Crossing the Atlantic Ocean.

women's suffrage In the United States, refers to the movement to win voting rights for women, which gathered strength in the 1840s and culminated with the ratification of the Nineteenth Amendment on August 18, 1920.

Chronology

1897 Amelia Earhart is born in Atchison, Kansas.

1908 Sees her the first plane at the Iowa State Fair, and is unimpressed.

1909 Earhart sisters leave Atchison and join their parents in Des Moines, Iowa.

1915 Amy Earhart moves to Chicago, Illinois, with her two daughters.

1916 Graduates from Hyde Park High School in Chicago.

1916 Attends Ogontz School outside of Philadelphia.

1917 During World War I, Earhart volunteers in Toronto as a nurse's assistant for wounded Canadian soldiers.

1918 The Spanish flu pandemic reaches Toronto. Earhart suffers from pneumonia and has minor sinus operations, which are not successful. She moves to her sister's home in Massachusetts and spends a year recovering. Earhart would have chronic sinusitis throughout her life.

1920 Earhart takes her first ride in an airplane.

1921 Attends her first flying lesson. Later that year, she passes her pilot's license tests and participates in the Pacific Coast Ladies' Derby.

1922 Unofficially, Earhart sets an altitude record for female pilots, flying her plane to 14,000 feet (4,627 m).

1923 Earhart becomes the sixteenth woman to receive her international pilot's license, allowing her to set records.

1927 Joins the Boston chapter of the National Aeronautic Association.

1928 Earhart is the first woman to fly across the Atlantic as a passenger. Her first book, *20 Hrs. 40 Min.*, is published.

1929 The Ninety-Nines is formed.

1931 George Putnam and Amelia Earhart marry and live in New York City. Earhart is elected the first president of the Ninety-Nines.

1932 Earhart becomes the first woman to fly solo across the Atlantic and becomes the first woman to receive the Distinguished Flying Cross. Her book *The Fun of It* is published. Earhart is the first woman to fly nonstop coast-to-coast across America.

1934 Receives the Harmon Trophy for America's Outstanding Airwoman for the third year in a row. Amelia Earhart Fashions is launched. Putnam and Earhart move to California.

1935 Sets three flying records for solo flights while working as a career counselor to women at Purdue University.

1937 Earhart makes two attempts to fly around the world. In July, during her second trip, her plane disappears; sixteen days later the United States calls off the search. Earhart's journal entries from the flight are published by Putnam in the book *Last Flight*.

1939 Though no body has been found, Earhart is declared dead.

1959 A woman claims that in 1937 she saw Japanese soldiers capture Earhart on the island of Saipan, and that Earhart was later executed.

1988 TIGHAR announces the Earhart Project, an endeavor to scientifically and conclusively solve Earhart's disappearance.

Further Information

Books

Flemming, Candace. *Amelia Lost: The Life and Disappearance of Amelia Earhart*. New York: Schwartz & Wade Books, 2011.

Haynsworth, Leslie, and David Toomey. *Earhart's Daughters*. New York: William Morrow and Company, 1998.

Vanhoenacker, Mark. *Skyfaring: A Journey with a Pilot*. New York: Alfred A. Knopf, 2015.

Websites

The Air Race Classic

http://www.airraceclassic.org

Follow the premier women pilots' air race, which happens annually.

The Eloquent Woman

http://eloquentwoman.blogspot.com/2012/03/famous-speech-friday-amelia-earhardts.html

Hear Earhart's voice as she delivers the speech "A Woman's Place in History" (or read a transcript of the speech).

Women of Aviation Worldwide Week

http://www.womenofaviationweek.org

This annual global outreach initiative raises awareness of aviation opportunities available to girls of all ages. It also is a time for celebrating the accomplishments of women of aviation. Plan your own activities or join in others!

Films

Earhart's Takeoff from Lae, New Guinea

https://www.youtube.com/watch?v=ntkOyDanuRw

Watch the last known film recording of Earhart, as she and Noonan board their plane to complete their around-the-world flight.

Bibliography

Adler, Jerry. "Will the Search for Amelia Earhart Ever End?" *Smithsonian*, January 2015. http://www.smithsonianmag.com/history/will-search-for-amelia-earhart-ever-end-180953646.

"Amelia Earhart Birthplace Museum." Amelia Earhart Museum. Accessed December 20, 2016. http://www.ameliaearhartmuseum.org/index.html.

"Amelia Earhart to Her Former Flight Instructor, Neta Snook, 1929." The Gilder Lehrman Institute of American History. Accessed December 20, 2016. https://www.gilderlehrman.org/history-by-era/roaring-twenties/resources/amelia-earhart-her-former-flight-instructor-neta-snook-192.

"Biography." AmeliaEarhart.com. Accessed December 20, 2016. http://www.ameliaearhart.com/about/bio.html.

Bryner, Jeanna. "Mystery Deepens Over Bones Linked to Amelia Earhart." *Live Science*, November 4, 2016. http://www.livescience.com/56752-castaway-bones-linked-to-amelia-earhart-questioned.html.

"Dick Rutan, Jeana Yeager, and the Flight of the Voyager." Centennial of Flight. Accessed December 20, 2016. http://www.centennialofflight.net/essay/Explorers_Record_Setters_and_Daredevils/rutan/EX32.htm.

Diliberto, Gioia. "Flights of Fashion: How Amelia Earhart Became America's First Celebrity Designer." *Huffington Post*.

Last updated May 25, 2011. http://www.huffingtonpost.com/gioia-diliberto/flights-of-fashion_b_240168.html.

Earhart, Amelia. Letter to George Putnam, February 7, 1931. Purdue University archives. http://earchives.lib.purdue.edu/cdm/singleitem/collection/earhart/id/2988.

"Famous Speech Friday: Amelia Earhart's 'A Woman's Place in Science.'" *The Eloquent Woman* (blog), March 30, 2012. http://eloquentwoman.blogspot.com/2012/03/famous-speech-friday-amelia-earhardts.html.

Grady, Denise. "American Woman Who Shattered Space Ceiling." *New York Times*, July 23, 2012. http://www.nytimes.com/2012/07/24/science/space/sally-ride-trailblazing-astronaut-dies-at-61.html.

"Jonahed." Wright Brothers Aeroplane Company. Accessed December 20, 2016. http://www.wright-brothers.org/History_Wing/Wright_Story/Inventing_the_Airplane/Jonahed/Jonahed.htm.

Marshall, Patti. "Anita Neta Snook." Historynet.com, March 12, 2012. http://www.historynet.com/anita-neta-snook.htm?PageSpeed=noscript.

"Patricia Cowings, PhD, NASA Psychophysiologist." *gradPSYCH*, September 2005. http://www.apa.org/gradpsych/2005/09/cover-cowings.aspx.

Phelan, Ben. "Navigating the Truth Behind Amelia Earhart and Fred Noonan." *Antiques Roadshow*, September 29, 2014. http://www.pbs.org/wgbh/roadshow/stories/articles/2014/9/29/navigating-truth-behind-amelia-earhart-and-fred-noonan.

"Ruby Wine Sheldon." *Arizona Republic*, November 30, 2012, quoted on Legacy.com. http://www.legacy.com/obituaries/azcentral/obituary.aspx?pid=161328667.

Spaleta, Steve. "Astronaut Peggy Whitson: Chicken Entrepreneur to Space Station Commander." Space.com, November 16, 2016. http://www.space.com/34741-astronaut-peggy-whitson-from-chicken-entrepreneur-to-space-station-commander-video.html.

Sullivan, Patricia. "Pioneering Pilot Elinor Smith Sullivan Dies at 98." *Washington Post*, March 24, 2010. http://www.washingtonpost.com/wp-dyn/content/article/2010/03/23/AR2010032303758.html.

"Thaden, Louise Mcphetridge." The National Aviation Hall of Fame. Accessed December 20, 2016. http://www.nationalaviation.org/our-enshrinees/thaden-louise-mcphetridge.

Thurman, Judith. "Missing Woman." *New Yorker*, September 14, 2009. http://www.newyorker.com/magazine/2009/09/14/missing-woman.

"Women in Aviation and Space History." Smithsonian National Air and Space Museum. Accessed December 20, 2016. https://airandspace.si.edu/explore-and-learn/topics/women-in-aviation/.

"Wright Brothers' Flying Machine." *NOVA*, September 2003. http://www.pbs.org/wgbh/nova/wright/reporter.html.

Index

Page numbers in **boldface** are illustrations. Entries in **boldface** are glossary terms.

About the Author

Kristin Thiel is a writer and editor. Her first book with Cavendish Square was on Dorothy Hodgkin, a Nobel Prize–winning chemist and pioneer in X-ray crystallography. Thanks in part to Amelia Earhart, air travel is no longer a big deal, and Thiel has made good use of that. When she was a student, she studied in places as varied as Ireland and South Africa; inspired by those experiences, she continues to take classes in other countries, even though she's no longer working toward a degree. She's grateful she has a phone with awesome GPS technology, or she'd always be lost. Sometimes she settles for exploring the world from her home in Portland, Oregon, reading other people's stories of traveling, her purring cat on her lap.